Chesapeake
Charlie
and
BLACKBEARD'S
TREASURE

Chesapeake Charlie
and
BLACKBEARD'S
TREASURE

WILLIAM L. COLEMAN

Bethany Fellowship INC.
MINNEAPOLIS, MINNESOTA 55438

Chesapeake Charlie and Blackbeard's Treasure
William L. Coleman

Library of Congress Catalog Card Number 80-70573
ISBN 0-87123-116-6

Published by Bethany Fellowship, Inc.
6820 Auto Club Road, Minneapolis, Minnesota 55438

Printed in the United States of America

A special thanks
to June Coleman for reading the manuscript
and to Mary Coleman for typing it.

Other Books by the Same Author

Devotional Series

Counting Stars
Listen to the Animals
My Magnificent Machine
On Your Mark
The Good Night Book
More About My Magnificent Machine
Today I Feel Like a Warm Fuzzy

Chesapeake Charlie Series

Chesapeake Charlie and the Bay Bank Robbers
Chesapeake Charlie and Blackbeard's Treasure

About the Author

WILLIAM L. COLEMAN is a graduate of the Washington Bible College in Washington, D.C., and Grace Theological Seminary in Winona Lake, Indiana. He has pastored three churches: a Baptist Church in Michigan, a Mennonite Church in Kansas, and an Evangelical Free Church in Aurora, Nebraska. He is a Staley Foundation Lecturer. The author of seventy-five magazine articles, his by-line has appeared in *Christianity Today*, *Eternity*, *Good News Broadcaster*, *Campus Life*, *Moody Monthly*, *Evangelical Beacon*, and *The Christian Reader*. This is his ninth children's book.

Chapter One

Mrs. Warren had been out of the classroom for a dangerously long time. No one was sure why the principal had called her away, but everyone was getting restless. Some were even feeling adventurous.

"Kerry! Kerry," Charlie warned, "you'd better get to your seat before she comes."

With a silly grin, Kerry Blake refused to move. He sat smugly on a chair next to the back wall.

"I'm the King of Biology," Kerry announced with a raised fist. "When Mrs. Warren returns, she'll obey my every command."

Most of the students ignored him. They were beginning to talk loudly, move desks, and throw paper wads. Chesapeake Charlie and Laura kept their eyes on Kerry.

They gave each other a knowing glance and suddenly bounced out of their seats like pogo sticks. "Yahoo!" Charlie yelled as he beat Laura to the back. Without hesitating he flew into the air and landed squarely on Kerry's lap. In one motion he threw his left arm around the startled king's neck.

Laura was only a step behind. In a single second she grabbed Charlie's shoulders and pulled him backwards.

"Hey!" he yelled, and his feet went straight up like

a stiff board. As they shot into the air, Charlie's feet caught the bottom of the silver-colored fire extinguisher, knocking it from its hook.

Bang! It hit the floor like a cannon shot. The surprised students whirled to see water gushing out of the old extinguisher and spewing over the room. Charlie struggled to his feet. Like Captain Marvel he ran toward the little tin volcano.

Courageously he grabbed the hose and tried to kink it. The hard rubber refused to budge. He choked it harder. As he struggled frantically the shower swept across the ceiling, splattering the windows and soaking the science equipment.

"Turn it upside down!" Kerry shouted. Swis-sh— Charlie accidentally hit Kerry in the face with the spray. Covering his head, Kerry charged forward.

Poor Laura hid behind the chair that had been Kerry's throne.

Kerry reached the extinguisher, picked it up and turned it on its head.

"It still won't stop!" Charlie yelled. As he pivoted toward Kerry, he unknowingly swung the small hose toward the students in the far corner of the room. They screamed and ran in all directions. Some dove under desks. One boy pulled the geography map down over his head.

Putt, putt, putt, putt, swi-ss-h. The extinguisher exhausted itself.

Charlie and Kerry looked around at the dripping room. Drops fell from the ceiling, the window shades, and the light fixtures. Desks were covered with a film of water.

"Aaah!" A scream of horror pierced the damp stillness. Mrs. Warren had returned.

"My mom says it was all your fault, Charlie." Kerry kept arguing as Charlie checked his crab lines.

"I know what your mom thinks." Charlie tried to stay calm as they walked around the pier.

"She says I shouldn't have had to stay after school, that I shouldn't have had to clean up the room."

"I've already heard all of this, Kerry." Charlie pulled up a string and checked his chicken-wing bait. A crab had been nibbling but had escaped.

"Well, have you heard this?" Kerry became loud. "My mom says we aren't going to pay one dime."

"Kerry!" Charlie said sternly, glaring nose-to-nose at Kerry. "You're scaring my crabs. Anyway, we both know whose fault it was. If Laura had stayed in her seat, none of this would have happened. Send the bill to Laura's parents. Hold it! I've got a nibble."

Charlie crouched down and grasped the string in his left hand. He could see the wiggling outline of a crab in the water. Slowly, carefully he pulled the string up. His right hand gripped the long-handled net. The crab jumped away.

"Nuts," grumbled Charlie. "There. He's back. It's a jimmie!"

Jimmies, large males with bright blue claws, are the best crabs to catch. A jimmie has more meat than the smaller, female sooks.

"I've got him, I've got him," Charlie whispered as he swung his net toward the water. The net moved smoothly and quickly.

"Yahoo!" A shriek sliced through the air. Charlie jumped like a frightened frog. His string jerked and the jimmie took off. Charlie looked up. There was the face that often sent chills up his spine. It was Laura.

"I had a beautiful jimmie. I bet he was ten inches across."

"That's what you get," she said with a pout. "I heard you blaming that fire extinguisher thing on me."

"My mom says she's not paying," Kerry interrupted.

"I don't care what your mom says," Laura spit back. "You two did it. I barely touched Charlie's shoulders. It's a wonder I didn't catch fleas."

"We ought to throw you into the Bay." Charlie pointed his finger and lowered his voice to sound tough.

"Lay a hand on me and I'll karate both of you," she warned.

"What's that in the water?" asked Kerry.

"Don't try to trick me," said Laura. "I don't fool that easily." She spread her feet and held her hands stiffly, ready to battle.

"No, really. Is that a bottle floating?"

"Sure. It's got a cork in it," said Charlie.

"Well, don't stand there. Give me your net," Laura ordered. Anything to get their minds off the argument.

She grabbed the net and soon had the bottle safely on the pier. "Look at this," she laughed as she held it up. "Why do tourists buy these things? It's one of those bottles with a map in it. They pay two bucks for these dumb things."

Without hesitating she threw it back into the water.

"Why did you do that?" Charlie picked up his net.

"I wanna keep it. It's worth two bucks."

"Charlie the junk collector," said Laura. "I bet you still have your first pacifier."

"Buzz off," Charlie chirped, as he lifted the bottle out of the water.

"Don't be so pushy." Laura added, "I can help you with your lines."

Without waiting for a reply, she walked to one of his half-dozen lines and began to tug on it.

"Then I'm going home," said Kerry. "But don't forget what my mom said."

"We promise, Kerry," Charlie groaned. "We really promise."

At first they didn't talk much. Each pulled on a couple of lines. They would get a few bites soon. The sun was warm so Laura removed her blue windbreaker and red cap. She had started to grow out of the rough, tomboy stage. Sometimes she wanted to smile and be gentle to boys, but the rest of the time she wanted to knock their blocks off.

"Sometimes I wish I was a crab," Charlie said finally.

"Why? Would you like to walk sideways?"

"Nah, I just like those eyes," he continued. "The way they hang out on little sticks. A crab can see all the way around. He can look at a 360-degree angle without moving. Think how handy that would be."

"Especially when you play kick-the-can," Laura added. "You could see people sneaking up on you."

"If I were a beautiful blue crab, I wouldn't need to buy new clothes either," said Charlie. "They change their skeleton twenty, maybe twenty-five, times in a couple of years."

Charlie pulled up his line, but only minnows were

chewing on his chicken.

"Their shell doesn't grow—that's their skeleton," he explained, "but their body does. So maybe every couple of months they push off their shell and grow another one."

"They must feel funny without any protection."

"You bet, but their new skeleton grows back quickly. It's like getting a new suit of armor," said Charlie. "It's called molting."

"Don't you ever get tired of studying the Bay?" asked Laura.

"Nope. I'm going over some day to check out Tangier Island. Scientists say that place is losing 25 feet of shoreline a year." Charlie liked to throw out facts and figures.

"I've got one!" Charlie announced with enthusiasm. He pulled his net out of the water to reveal a dancing, large-clawed jimmie.

"Man, he's big," he added as he swung his net over to the bucket. Charlie flipped the net and tried to shake the crab loose. The creature stubbornly grasped the net. Charlie reached toward the net with his free, bare hand. Carefully he pushed his fingers against the crab's broad back. One mistake and the crab could snap Charlie's finger.

Cautiously Charlie pressed one finger and then a second. Snap! The monstrous claw took a swipe at the boy's hand. Charlie jerked it back and the crab locked firmly onto the net. Charlie tried several times and finally his catch broke loose and plopped into the bucket of water.

For the next hour neither Laura nor Charlie said much. They caught a few crabs, but most were small ones, which they threw back.

The evening was bringing a cool breeze off the Bay. It was time they started home.

"Laura," his voice surprised her. Charlie was standing next to her line.

"I'm sorry we gave you such a hard time." Charlie knelt beside her, trying to look as sincere as possible. "Here, you take the crabs home. You know, kind of a peace offering." His smile showed his healthy teeth.

"No, I couldn't do that," said Laura. "But you are nice to say you're sorry."

"Nah, I know sometimes I'm a heel and I say some pretty terrible things." Charlie dumped the crabs into one bucket and set that pail inside the empty one. "Let's face it, Laura, we're growing up. Girls and guys start to look at each other differently."

"Really?" she said. "I mean, sure they do."

"You bet, Laura." Charlie began walking away. "I can see why a guy could start liking someone like you."

Laura's grin was as wide as a super highway. As Charlie disappeared down the pier, she picked up her jacket and slipped it on. Charlie wouldn't be a little twerp all his life, she thought. He wasn't such a bad guy at that. And besides, he was far from being ugly. Laura planted her cap firmly on her head. She just felt good all over.

"O-u-ch!" she screamed. "Ouch, ouch!" Laura grabbed her cap and threw it onto the pier. "Ouch!" she repeated. Her hands reached up and felt a small, pesky crab in her hair. She hit it quickly with her stiff palm as she jumped up and down. The frightened creature fell to the pier and scurried over the side into the water.

"Charlie Dean!" she yelled. "You're the

u-g-l-i-e-s-t animal alive. I've seen better looking toads!"

Life was never boring for Chesapeake Charlie. If nothing exciting was happening, it didn't take him long to make it happen. Chesapeake Bay was his world of adventure. He was surrounded by animals, the water, storms, sunsets, and boats. Every shoreline, river, woods, and back road needed to be explored. Even the smells of the Bay were fascinating. Charlie loved the tangy aroma of the briny seaweed. His mind almost blew fuses when he smelled oyster fritters and crab cakes frying. Just the sight of butter melting on hot sweet potato biscuits was enough to stand his taste buds on end.

In the evenings when it was too dark to prod, investigate, and experiment in the outdoors, Chesapeake Charlie loved to pore over books about the Bay. He would read almost anything. Charlie knew about boats, history, pirates, famous storms, and fascinating heroes. He also read about the wildlife that helped make up his world.

"Come get some ice cream," Mrs. Dean called to her son. Charlie liked to read, but he also enjoyed people, animals, and ice cream. Especially ice cream.

The Dean family liked to make their own. Their gallon freezer had to be cranked by hand. Charlie and his younger brother Pete were always begging for an electric freezer. "It tastes better if you crank it by hand," their dad had said for maybe the thousandth time.

"Guess what I learned new." Charlie's mental wheels were still spinning when he sat at the table. He laid his book down and reached for the bowl his mother handed him. "Did you know there used to be real pirates in the Chesapeake Bay?"

"Oh, sure," his dad said matter-of-factly.

"You mean real pistol-packing, sword-swinging pirates?" asked Pete.

"You got it, Pete," Charlie assured. He poured rich, dark chocolate syrup over his ice cream. It slid down the sides of his cold vanilla mountain.

"Some say the mouth of the Bay was the most dangerous place on the east coast." He sprinkled on chopped nuts.

"Here and Long Island." Charlie stuffed banana slices around the sides of the delicious sundae. His mouth began to water as he talked.

"Not just little pipsqueaks but the famous pirates." He was busy shaking the whipped cream can. Charlie smothered his dessert with the sweet fluff.

"Fly and Vidal and Blackbeard all plundered in the Bay." Charlie crowned his creation with a huge, red strawberry. It was so irresistible he tossed on a second one.

"It must have been 250 years ago." Charlie buried his spoon in the cold mound of pure pleasure and drew out a heaping helping. The dark chocolate dripped off.

"Around 1710." The spoonful disappeared into his waiting mouth—except for some whipped cream that caught on his nose.

"It all sounds like a bunch of fairy tales to me," Pete scoffed. "Pirates were around the Virgin Islands. We had Indians here."

"That's true too," Mr. Dean volunteered. "But it's also true that there were plenty of pirates on the Bay.

Some people even believe Edward Teach sailed here."

"Edward Teach doesn't sound like a big pirate to me," Pete said, puzzled.

"That was Blackbeard's real name, dummy," said Charlie disgustedly.

"Did they hang him from the mast?" asked Pete.

"As the story goes," their dad continued, "Blackbeard was shot to death. They say he had twenty-five wounds in him—twenty from swords and knives and five from pistols."

"Gruesome," Mrs. Dean added with a shiver.

"But that's not all," Mr. Dean went on. "Then they cut off his head and swung it from the bowsprit of the Maynard."

"I would have chased the pirates across the Bay," Pete spouted as he thrust his spoon through the air like a sword. "Then I'd have captured their treasure and been rich."

"Maybe you still could," said Mr. Dean. "When I was your age the old folks used to say there was pirate treasure near here. They said some of the old writers claimed Blackbeard buried treasure close by."

"Has any of it been found?" asked Charlie.

"Not as far as I know," Mr. Dean explained. "But some of us used to look for it." He smiled.

"Were pirates really as mean as they say?" asked Pete.

"Of course they were," Charlie said smugly. "Weren't they, Dad?"

"Well, I don't know about all of them. I remember Blackbeard had four pirate ships and four hundred men under him. It must've been a terrible sight to sail around a bend in the Bay and see those four ships staring right at you. Each had the ugly Jolly Roger flag flying with its skull and crossbones."

"I'd have just outrun them," said Pete.

"Sometimes you could, but they were fast and usually not loaded down with cargo."

"Then I'd outfight them," said Pete.

"You are dense," Charlie insisted.

"They were terrifying fighters," Mr. Dean continued. "Blackbeard's men even made their own hand grenades. They stuffed wine bottles with gun powder, packed in small metal shot and maybe some scrap iron. They'd hang a fuse from the top, light it and start aboard your ship with the fuse burning—sword in one hand and a smoking grenade in the other."

"I'd have just gotten my machine gun out," said Pete.

"You're a chowder-head. They didn't have machine guns then," Charlie declared. "Didn't they have big cannons on board?"

"Absolutely," said Mr. Dean. "Back in school I saw pictures of one of his ships. If I remember correctly it had forty guns—twenty on each side. Can you imagine those blasting away at you?"

"Was Blackbeard a fighter or just a captain?" Charlie asked.

"I suppose you had to be a mean fighter to be a pirate captain. Again, from the drawings I've seen, he wore a huge bandolier across his chest. He carried three loaded and cocked pistols there. Then he had a wide belt around his waist packed with pistols, daggers, and swords. When he crossed over onto your vessel, he had all of this plus a pistol in one hand and a sword in the other.

"If there is buried treasure," asked Charlie, "why would a pirate bury it? I'd take it all and retire."

"But don't forget," said Mr. Dean, "pirates were greedy. They couldn't carry all their loot and they couldn't put it in the bank. They planned to come back and get it later. Unfortunately for Blackbeard, he didn't get back for most of it."

"Would it be valuable if someone found his treasure today?" Pete asked.

"Some certainly would," Mr. Dean explained. "There were clothes and food as well as furniture and gold. I wouldn't mind finding some myself."

"I might get a shovel and dig around a little," announced Pete.

"If you stretched all the shoreline of the Chesapeake Bay in one straight line," Charlie said, changing the subject, "how far do you think it would reach?"

"From here to Cleveland," Pete volunteered.

"Beats me," said Mr. Dean.

"From here all the way across the United States and into the Pacific Ocean," Charlie stretched his words. "That's 4,000 miles of shoreline."

"You really enjoy the Bay," said Mr. Dean.

"Try a quick quiz," Charlie continued.

Pete started to leave.

"It'll only take a minute. Where do the big crabs spend the winter?" asked Charlie.

"In the deep center of the Bay," Mr. Dean answered.

"How did you know that?"

"I've been around the Bay awhile myself," Mr. Dean answered with a wink.

"Whose turn is it to carry out the trash?" Mrs. Dean asked.

Pete hurried noiselessly out of the living room.

"I guess that answers that," teased Charlie.

"I was wondering," Mr. Dean began, but stopped in the middle of his sentence.

"Wondering what?" Charlie prodded.

"Well, I was wondering which you liked best—the Chesapeake summers or the winters?"

"Probably the summers, but the winters are interesting, too. Like when we went over to Lynnhaven to get those oysters."

"That was a fun trip," Mr. Dean commented.

"And the oysters were delicious," said Charlie. "Not as good as ours, but Virginia oysters aren't bad."

"There is a different flavor to Lynnhaven oysters," said Mr. Dean.

"I heard that Diamond Jim Brady of New York was so wealthy he often had Lynnhaven oysters shipped to him. They say he'd eat two to three dozen at a sitting."

"They have an excellent reputation," Mr. Dean agreed.

"I bet Diamond Jim was a pudgy fellow," Charlie said with a chuckle.

Then he added with a faraway tone, "You know, I think I enjoy every season on the Bay."

Chapter Two

"Boo!"

"Hey!" Charlie jerked around like a surprised thief.

"Don't get so jumpy," said Kerry.

"How did you get down here?" growled Charlie. He turned his back against the workbench.

"No one answered my knock so I just followed the sound of your drill into the basement."

"Well, this is private territory so you'd better leave," Charlie warned sternly.

"Does your mom know you're drilling on her coffee table?" Kerry could see the brown leg poking out around Charlie.

"I am not," Charlie lied.

"Now your nose is going to grow."

"Nuts," Charlie sputtered. "Kerry, I'm going to tell you this, but you are the only person who knows. If anyone else ever finds out, I'll tell your mom what happened to her good panty hose."

"It's a deal, Charlie."

"Come here. I take this long drill bit and drill a hole straight up each leg of the table. They have to be perfectly straight. Then I use the legs for my bank. I have about five dollars in dimes in each leg. I bought these corks and they fit perfectly. Even if you turn the table over you won't notice them.

"C-o-o-l, man." Kerry was wide-eyed. "Is this the only table you use for a bank?"

"You think I'm a fool? Good hiders never tell. But you can be sure geniuses have plenty of ideas."

"Laura was right. You do have a lot of junk in your basement." Kerry looked around at the stacks of boxes, piles of tin, neat coils of wire, and posters of football players spread across the walls.

"Do you still collect baseball cards?" asked Kerry.

"When I can get them," said Charlie as he picked up his drill and continued his project.

"Hey!" Kerry tried to yell over the sound of the drill. "How much you want for that old tiger skin?"

"Nope," he answered without stopping. "They're too hard to get."

"It's fake anyway," Kerry insisted.

"Maybe not," Charlie argued.

"Is too."

"Well, it looks real. Besides, I like it on my wall. It reminds me that I'm going big game hunting some day."

"It sure is dull around here," Kerry bellowed.

"Won't be for long," said Charlie.

"What do you mean?"

"Because of that bait bucket. Don't touch it, but as soon as I get these dimes in I've got a terrific idea."

Kerry went over and kicked gently against the tin bucket. Whatever was in it made a strange scratching sound.

"There! I've got it," Charlie announced. He held the coffee table high to make sure the corks were even. Then he placed it firmly on the floor.

"Remember," he pointed at Kerry, "never a word of this."

"Scout's honor," Kerry mocked as he held up three fingers.

"You grab the bait bucket and I'll take the table."

"Okay! Say, you still have that bottle?" asked Kerry.

"You bet. It even has an old date on it—1703. Tourists will believe anything," Charlie laughed. "But wait 'til they see what's in the bucket."

"Keep low," whispered Charlie. They had cut through the woods and arrived three quarters of a mile south of Charlie's house. "No one will see us under the pier."

Three young children were playing near the shore but none noticed the two boys. Five small, white cottages were lined up like soldiers. Each was short, wide and had a screened-in porch.

"Don't worry," said Charlie. "We'll just scare those kids and shake up some tourists."

Charlie removed the lid and took out a small alligator. All eight inches were twisting and wiggling. It tried to snap its long, toothy jaws but didn't have enough power to make a sound.

"These were the last three the pet shop had," said Charlie. He handed the second to Kerry and took the third for himself.

"You sure they won't bite the kids?" asked Kerry.

"No chance, but I bet they'll sure scare 'em. Let's stay and watch their faces."

All three were placed just beyond the weeds and pointed directly toward the cottages and the children.

One of the green creatures started to veer to the left. Frantically Kerry's hand darted out and grabbed the alligator. In one swift motion he twisted the creature around and aimed it toward the target.

Slowly the trio ambled along. Charlie and Kerry crouched like spies, watching their journey. The alligator on the left stopped suddenly and opened its mouth wide.

"What's that ugly lizard up to?" Kerry asked, not expecting an answer. The words were hardly out before they saw a grasshopper leap over the alligator's mouth.

"That grasshopper's lucky," said Charlie. "Al, the alligator, would have torn him apart." They both chuckled.

"There goes Hector." Kerry pointed to the one on the right. "He's heading south again."

Kerry started to race from under the pier, but Charlie grabbed his ankle.

"Stay put!" Charlie commanded. "We'll just have to let him go."

"Woof, woof."

"It's a dog," said Kerry.

"Woof, woof."

"He's coming toward the 'gators."

"So is one of the kids."

The boy couldn't have been more than four. He stood beside the barking dog and watched the two remaining alligators. They opened their mouths like old scissors, trying hard to look ferocious.

Without hesitating the boy reached down and took an alligator in his left hand. In a quick sweep he had the second in his right. He ran toward one of the cottages. The dog kept barking as if he were fighting off an invasion of Martians.

"Maybe we'd better beat it." Kerry took a step to leave.

"Not yet," said Charlie. "The fun has just begun."

Wap! The screen door of the cottage smacked against the porch as it swung open. The man standing in the door in bathing shorts and a white T-shirt looked a great deal like an angry father. He gripped the shotgun in his hands as if he were about to kill someone.

"Let's get out of here," said Kerry.

"It's too late. He'll see us. Stay low."

Booooom! The shotgun blasted into the air, startling children, birds, the dog, and two quiet characters shaking under the pier.

"Alligators! Alligators!" the man yelled.

"Now tell me this wasn't your idea." Kerry's face looked pained.

"Don't panic." Charlie tried to look calm. "We can still get out of this."

Wap, wap. Screen doors were slamming and people pouring out of the cottages.

"Alligators? Where?" said one man carrying a long broom handle. The woman beside him held a shiny butcher knife. Six or eight people of different ages and sizes had assembled. One boy held a baseball bat and a catcher's mask.

"Now, wait a minute." The manager had arrived and hoped to settle everyone down.

"We're being attacked by alligators!" the dad declared.

"There must be some mistake," the manager insisted. "There are no alligators in the Chesapeake Bay."

"That's what you say," said the dad. "Two of them just tried to eat my son. Everyone spread out. We'll march to the water in a straight line."

Each of the volunteers moved over until they were about twenty feet from their nearest partner.

"This is ridiculous!" shouted the manager.

"If you don't want to help us, stand aside," said the dad. "Attention! March!"

Bravely they stepped forward. A shotgun, a broom handle, a baseball bat, a butcher knife, a crab net, a scuba spear, and a bucket—all in different stages of readiness.

"They're coming straight toward us," Kerry said shakily.

"Keep cool. I'll think of something."

"They think there's an alligator under the pier." Kerry was ready to run.

Tramp, tramp, tramp. The boys could hear the footsteps as the make-shift army stepped high and cautiously across the grassy beach.

"Let's swim out."

"Not yet," said Charlie.

"That man's got a shotgun!"

The vacationers had moved halfway from the cottages toward the water.

"All right. On three we swim for it," said Charlie. "One, two—"

"Aaah!" The scream came from the lady with the butcher knife. As her blood-curdling shriek rang out, she pivoted and collapsed to the ground in a dead faint.

The rest of the army hurried to her side. There in her path they saw a third baby alligator thrusting its menacing teeth toward them. Thump. Someone dumped a bucket over the mini-monster.

"Alligators! Alligators!" the leader bellowed.

Meanwhile two frightened boys raced through the woods without as much as a glance backwards.

"I don't know when I have heard so much excitement over nothing," Charlie's dad said that evening as they sat in the living room. "That news story on the radio about alligators in the Bay. Everybody knows 'gators don't live in the Bay."

"That's right," said Charlie. This was one discussion he didn't care to get involved in.

"Now someone's trying to organize an alligator hunt. They say the State Patrol is being flooded with calls from people reporting sightings. How could some fairy tale like this get started?

"Last year it was Bigfoot, then it was UFO's. Now they're looking for Al, the alligator."

Charlie never looked up from his magazine.

"Guess what I'm going to do," Charlie spoke up to change the subject.

"What's that?" asked Mr. Dean to be polite.

"I'm going to train a crab for the Crisfield Derby."

"I think you'd enjoy that." Mr. Dean continued reading his newspaper.

"If I train it just right, he'll become the most famous crab in America. This is the way I figure it. The crabs are dumped onto a wooden board and they take off for the finish line. If I could teach a blue crab that when he is gently dropped onto a board there is food around, he'll run for it."

"Sounds goofy," said Pete.

"Sounds all right to me," Mr. Dean encouraged.

"Maybe I'll even enter the Governor's Cup for foreign crabs. Bet we could beat those Hawaiian Warriors."

"I'm not sure of that, or even if they'd let you enter," said Mr. Dean. "Anyway, you have till Labor Day."

"If Crisfield is still around on Labor Day," Charlie kidded.

"Where can Crisfield go?" asked Pete.

"Most of the town is sitting on old oyster shells," said Charlie. "If they ever shift, the downtown will probably collapse."

"Towns don't collapse, do they, Dad?" asked Pete.

"Not generally. It is true that Crisfield is sitting on oyster shells, though. A hundred years ago they used to shuck oysters and dump the shells into the marsh. After a while places were packed with shells, maybe five and six feet deep. Finally the city just started building on top of the shells.

If the buildings haven't collapsed yet, they aren't very likely to."

"Sure," said Charlie. "But they could."

"Is that your bottle in the basement, Charlie?" asked Mrs. Dean.

"The green one?" Charlie sounded surprised.

"It's an odd looking thing," she continued.

"'Oh, it's just a gimmick. They sell them to tourists." Charlie shrugged it off.

"It must be more than that," she explained. "The shape and color are unusual, plus that number on the bottom—1-7-0-3. It looks different to me."

"I haven't seen the bottle, but it's easy enough to find out. Woody has a small collection of bottles at the store," said Mr. Dean. "He could probably tell you if it's worth a few bucks."

"Shhh," said Pete sitting in front of the television. "I'm trying to watch 'The Green Blob Eats Seattle.' "

That night Charlie quietly smuggled the bottle to his room. His curiosity was beginning to drive him mad. He had never even bothered to look at the map inside.

The cork was tight and dark. No matter how hard he struggled, it wouldn't twist either way. Finally he decided to take drastic measures. He took his penknife from the drawer. After five minutes of chipping away, the cork sliced into bits and the bottle surrendered its treasure.

With a little pushing, Charlie's smallest finger barely reached the paper and it slid out with ease. He opened the crisp, yellowed roll. It was no larger than half a sheet of paper and unrolled effortlessly like a loose scroll.

Charlie had no trouble recognizing the map. Drawn neatly in black ink, it was an excellent sketch of the Easton, St. Michaels area of the Chesapeake Bay. Some of the names were different and the spelling was odd, but he knew the territory.

Several things practically leaped off the page at Charlie. One was the skull and crossbones drawn in the right-hand corner. The second feature was a large X marked next to a tree on one of the small islands.

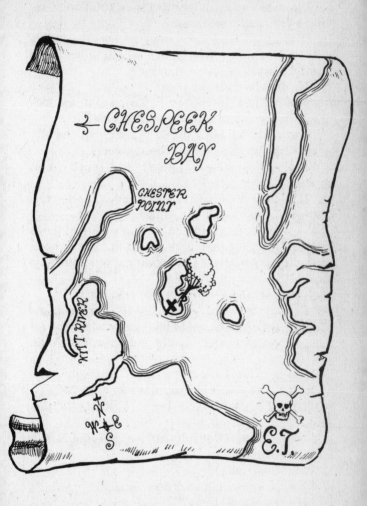

Then in neat and fancy printing were two letters under the skull and crossbones: E. T.

"Good morning, Woody." Charlie tried to sound cheerful and casual at the same time.

"Hi, Charlie. Can I help you?"

"N-a-h. I just dropped by to buy a soda." He took a hefty swallow from his bottle. "Been busy?"

"Not bad," said Woody. "I heard about the alligator scare. Anything for a little excitement."

"Hello, Charlie Dean." A soft voice called his attention.

"Hide your fire extinguisher, Woody. The destroyer is here," Charlie said sarcastically.

"Don't be cute," said Laura. "I was down at the library to tape some records this morning. You do know what a library is, don't you? What are you up to anyway?"

"Just drinking a soda," he answered curtly.

"I'm sure it would be thrilling to stand here and chit-chat with a brilliant lad like you, but I have to get these groceries home." Laura used her haughtiest voice.

"Rev it up and head it out," said Charlie.

Without another word Laura left for home.

"How long have you been collecting bottles, Woody?"

"I don't know if I'd really call it a collection. I have seven or eight."

"May I see them?"

"Sure, they're right back here."

"How do you get them?"

"Depends. Some I traded for and some I bought at auctions."

"They look neat. I won't touch any."

"Bottles are worth a little but not too much. This one is my best. It's Dr. Townsend's sarsaparilla. It's olive green and has these tears—they're bubbles of air in the glass. It's probably worth about $75."

"Where did you get Hall's Hair Renewer?"

"Bought it at an auction. They're rare. Especially with the fancy tops."

"What's the oldest bottle you've ever seen?"

They walked back to the front of the store.

"I think 1860," said Woody. "A lot of bottles were broken during the Civil War."

"Did they have bottles back in 1703?"

"Certainly. We've had bottles for thousands of years. Old ones are rare, but once in a while one will pop up. Not too many years ago a dozen bottles were recovered from a shipwreck off the coast of England. They were dated back to the 1700's."

"This will sound like a silly question, but I've often wondered, did pirates really put maps in bottles?"

"Who can say for sure?" said Woody. "I haven't seen many pirate maps, but I can imagine a pirate captain putting a map in a bottle and hiding it in his private whiskey collection in his cabin. As long as he was alive it would be his. The big pirates probably had a few maps here and a few maps there."

"What would you do," asked Charlie, "if you happened to buy one at an auction or something?"

"It's unlikely, but the bottle is probably worth $150 or more. Don't tell me you're going to start hunting for bottles?"

"It's a possibility," said Charlie. "Is there any way to know if a bottle is really old?"

"Well, of course some bottles will have a date on

them, but not many. Otherwise you have to check the shape, the opening, and the type of glass."

"Thanks, Woody. You're a big help."

"Oh, really? Why did you want to know?"

"You never know—I might start collecting bottles."

As Charlie hurried out the door Laura almost bumped into him.

"Leaving so soon?" she asked.

"Have to. I've got things to do you'd never understand." Charlie kept moving.

"I didn't expect to see you again so soon," said Woody.

"Oh, I forgot something. I think I left it right here by the flour sacks. Yes, here it is."

"You don't want to lose a nice tape recorder like that."

"No, sir." Laura proudly held it tightly to her chest.

Charlie went directly to his room without a word. Digging through the bottom drawer, he lifted his bottle from under his sweat shirts.

Where was that date? Right on the back of the bottle near the bottom. 1703. That must be it. It was the only thing written on the glass.

Reaching over to his bookshelf, Charlie removed his large book of maps. He turned to his map of the Chesapeake Bay and quickly pulled the paper from his bottle.

"They have to match," he thought as his fingers fumbled across the paper. Charlie checked and rechecked. This section looked like the Andrews River.

That part looked like the Smith Bend. But rivers and bays change over hundreds of years. How could he be certain?

"There," Charlie whispered aloud, "it's Randolph Island. The X is marked on the south side of Randolph Island."

He gently pushed the map back into the bottle and placed it in the drawer. Charlie leaned back on his bed and began to daydream. How should he go about organizing a real treasure hunt?

Unable to sleep, Charlie's mind raced in every direction. There were so many things he wanted to do and places he was determined to see. Most of his thoughts centered on the fascinating Bay he thoroughly enjoyed.

After lying restlessly for some time, he reached for some of the books by his bed. Charlie shuffled through a couple copies of Encyclopedia Brown. He really liked that character. His book about famous football players was only half finished.

Charlie's parents subscribed to two magazines about the Chesapeake Bay. The magazines spent most of their time in Charlie's room. Each issue was worn ragged from being read over and over.

None of the books seemed interesting at the moment. Then his eye caught his light green Bible. Charlie reached over and picked it up.

Charlie wouldn't qualify as one of the world's great Bible readers, but every few nights he picked it up. The Proverbs were his favorite part. That and the life of Christ. After reading a couple of pages his eyes closed and Charlie was sleeping with his clothes and light both on.

Chapter Three

"Hand me that stethoscope." Charlie motioned toward the cabinet.

"Where did you get this?" Kerry asked as he lifted the black, wobbly medical instrument.

"At Blake's Junk Shop," replied Charlie as he began to tie the metal end inside a large coffee can.

"Ha, ha. Well, I might as well ask you. I know I'll be sorry. What in the world are you making?"

"It's my official invention. But you will only laugh if I tell you," Charlie answered.

"I won't laugh," Kerry said impatiently.

"I call it 'Charlie's Fish Conversation Finder.' When I place it on the bottom of a boat, I will be able to hear fish talk."

"Ha, ha, ha, ha, ha, ha!" Kerry roared.

"You said you wouldn't laugh," Charlie said sternly.

"You didn't say it was going to be this funny." Kerry burst into a second roar. He doubled half over and smacked his knee.

Charlie looked serious. "You don't believe fish can talk, do you?"

"I never heard one." Kerry wiped his eyes with his hands.

"Of course you know dolphins talk all the time.

Did you happen to know that Bay Marine scientists insist that fish talk?"

"Whatever you say, Charlie."

"When I get it rigged up I might even make a record of a white perch singing." Charlie put his listening equipment on the brown cabinet.

"Probably sell a million." Kerry was still giggling.

Suddenly changing his mood, Charlie leaned toward Kerry.

"Can you keep a secret?"

"Sure."

"Would you like to make some big money?"

"How?"

"Do you think you can trust me?"

"I—I think so."

"You can't *think* so. You have to trust me."

"My mom warned me not to trust you."

"I'm not asking your mother. Do *you* trust me?"

"I suppose."

Charlie looked around his backyard to make sure no one was listening. Everything was still. Even the boats were motionless on the Bay.

"I'll need some insurance," said Charlie.

"Insurance?"

"I have to have it. I'm talking big money and you'll get twenty percent."

"Twenty percent? Why not half?"

"Because I know where the money is, and I'm talking big money."

"What kind of insurance?"

"Well—bring me five dollars."

"Five bucks? Forget it."

"You'll get it back—unless you tell the secret. I

also want a note that promises you will never tell this secret."

"Big money, Kerry, big money. You get back here in ten minutes with five bucks. I'll take care of the paper for the note. If you're late I may get somebody else."

Kerry took off in a full run, while Charlie went into the house. He collected a piece of paper, a bottle of lemon juice, and a tiny paint brush. By the time he had returned to the porch, Kerry was back and panting hard. His hand was filled with three bills and the rest in change.

"Are you sure it's big money?" asked Kerry.

"You've got to trust me, Kerry. Now take this brush and dip it into the lemon juice."

Kerry obeyed.

"Now write, 'I will keep this secret.' "

"It's hard with a brush."

"You can do it. Write the date and sign it."

Charlie took the note and blew on the drying lemon juice.

"Now it's our secret. No one will think to hold this up to the light and read it." Charlie folded the note and pushed it into his pocket with the five dollars.

"What secret? You haven't told me anything."

"Okay, listen carefully." Charlie took one more glance around the yard and then started to whisper to Kerry.

By early afternoon their plan was beginning to take shape. Charlie had moved his white rowboat off its rack and pulled it to shore. Kerry had collected two shovels and a metal detector. They added a small basket of strawberries to their supplies.

"If we get this detector wet, Uncle Ben will have my hide," said Kerry. "I've got to return it before he gets home tomorrow."

"Don't worry. We can buy your uncle a dozen metal detectors when we're done. Put this box near the bow. Without it we're out of business. These are cookies, and this is to give us energy." Charlie handed Kerry an eight pack of soda.

"No, Throckmorton." Charlie used his roughest voice. The large brown beagle stopped and drooped its head. "You can't come this time." Throckmorton always appeared a little sad, but now he looked as if he might cry. He began to whine softly.

"We might need him," said Kerry. "He makes a tough watchdog."

Throckmorton picked up an orange life jacket in his mouth and stood wagging his tail.

"Sometimes he looks almost human," Charlie said. "All right, but you have to wear the life jacket. The Bay is too deep out toward the middle."

Kerry and Charlie slipped the jacket over Throckmorton's front legs. Charlie then lay on the ground and began to tie the strings. Throckmorton licked Charlie's face.

"Stop that."

"Throckmorton's the only dog I know who would wear a life preserver," Kerry marveled.

"He knows that's the only way I'll take him that far in the boat."

"I told Mom I'd be late getting back, but I didn't say what our secret was."

"That's good. Let's push out."

"Have fun, boys," a voice sang behind them.

Charlie and Kerry both stopped at the sound of that voice.

"Hope you catch a lot of fish." Laura strolled slowly toward the boat. "Well, my, my," she said, "you forgot your fishing equipment! I bet you're glad I noticed that. Or were you going to catch fish with that metal detector?"

"It's none of your business." The boys went back to pushing the boat.

"That's fine with me. I'm going inside to play this for your mother, Charlie." Laura patted her tape recorder.

"So-oo-oo?" Charlie didn't want to discuss it, but he wondered.

"The tape might explain to her where you're going."

"What are you talking about?" Both boys turned to face her.

"Oh, maybe you would like to hear some of it?" She pushed the "play" button.

"How long have you been collecting bottles, Woody?" the recorder said. "I don't know if I'd really call it a collection. I have seven or eight."

"Where did you get that?" Charlie demanded, fuming.

"I have my ways."

"That's illegal. Give me that," he ordered.

"Not so quick. I had that bottle before you guys."

"But you threw it back."

"Nevertheless I did own it. It looks like you dim lights are going treasure hunting. You will obviously need an extra brain."

"Forget it. We don't take sneaks along," said Kerry.

"Fine. If you are going to cheat me out of my treasure, I'll just have to tell everyone what I've seen and heard."

"Get a life preserver," Charlie groaned. "Everyone's out to get me."

All four soon piled into the boat and cast off.

"Don't worry, I can find Randolph Island," said Laura, sitting in the bow of the boat.

"Shhh, you don't have to tell the whole world," said Charlie. He and Kerry were rowing. Throckmorton stood in the stern, his orange life jacket bright in the afternoon sun.

"Pull harder," barked Charlie.

"It's not my fault," Kerry whined.

"Row to the starboard!" shouted Laura. "Pull to the port."

Each stroke of the oars strained the boys' muscles. After an hour and a half of rowing, their shoulders ached and their arms felt like rubber. Throckmorton stood motionless except to occasionally poke his nose at a fish in the water. Laura managed to sit erect in the bow and continue to bark orders.

"I see land!" Laura called out as if she were Columbus sighting the West Indies. She stood up causing the boat to rock. "Full speed ahead. Row faster. Lay the whip to their backs." The boys looked at each other with anger and rowed harder.

"It's Randolph Island," Laura announced.

"It looks halfway between a hammock and a thump," said Charlie.

"A what and a where?" asked Kerry.

"A hammock and a thump," Charlie repeated. "A hammock is a large island with trees and houses. A thump is a tiny island with just one tree or none. This one is halfway between."

"That must make it a hamthump," Laura roared with laughter.

"How can you live on the Bay and not speak the language?" Charlie said disgustedly.

The trio gazed ahead at a small tree-dotted island covered with tall grass. Its shores were high from erosion. Otherwise the island was bare except for a large abandoned lighthouse that stood in the middle like a crown.

"What a neat old building," said Charlie.

Kerry's mouth dropped open and Laura was speechless. Throckmorton couldn't even bark.

"We'll have to check this out," Charlie told them.

In fifteen minutes they had safely beached the boat and tied its rope around a small tree growing at an angle out of the bank. It didn't take them long to pull off their preservers and climb up the bank. Charlie and Kerry hauled the shovels while Laura lugged the metal detector.

"Let's look at this map," said Charlie as he dropped his shovel and reached inside his shirt. "The X is marked next to a large tree on the south side of the island."

They looked toward the south.

"But there are three large trees. Looks like they've been here hundreds of years," said Kerry.

"Doesn't the map tell which tree?" asked Laura.

"It only shows one. I suppose Blackbeard remembered which tree. But he didn't have a metal detector. It won't take us long to find the treasure." Charlie picked up his shovel and led the march toward the first tree.

Laura began to comb the ground with the detector. Her earphones were in place ready to pick up the slightest signal.

This wasn't Throckmorton's idea of fun, so he roamed around the island. His detective nose kept taking him closer to the huge, old, wooden lighthouse. The six-sided house had been worn badly from the rough weather and neglect. Many of its windows were broken out and a door hung on one hinge. It creaked as the wind blew against it. On top of the main structure there stood a special room completely surrounded by windows. Lights had shone there to warn sailors of the dangerous rocks and shallow water.

Throckmorton's nose led him inside.

"I can't get a beep," said Laura as she took her earphones off.

"It's probably buried too deep for that gadget," Charlie reasoned. "Here, you two start digging." He pushed his shovel toward Laura.

"Why me?" She pulled her arm back.

"Captains don't dig," Charlie said with authority.

"Well it's my metal detector," Kerry complained. "I shouldn't have to dig."

"It's your uncle's metal detector," said Charlie. "Your uncle doesn't have to dig. Dig!" he shouted.

Kerry and Laura grumbled, but they began their hard job. Kerry's muscles were already stretched to their limit from rowing. Each shovelful made his arms ache.

"You know what pirates did to their diggers, don't you?" teased Charlie.

"Gave them chests full of gold?" Kerry hoped.

"Nope. They shot them. That way they couldn't come back and steal the treasure. Don't worry, I only plan to wound you two." Charlie laughed loudly, but his two friends didn't.

"Woof, woof."

"Throckmorton must have found something," Laura remarked.

"Probably a rabbit." Charlie tried to shrug it off.

"Woof, woof." Throckmorton pulled at Charlie's pant leg.

"Back off, boy." Charlie pushed at the dog's head.

"Woof, woof."

"He sounds urgent," said Kerry.

Throckmorton rose onto his back legs and pushed both of his front paws against Charlie's stomach.

"Hey, watch it. Hey, hey!" Charlie stumbled backwards and fell into the hole they were digging. He landed flat on his seat and sat looking stunned.

"It must be more than a rabbit." Charlie climbed out of the small hole. "I'm going to see what it is."

Throckmorton ran ahead and the trio of treasure hunters followed. The beagle took them straight to the creaking door of the lighthouse.

"It's dark in here," warned Kerry. "Let's wait 'til we get flashlights."

"Don't be chicken," said Charlie. He swallowed hard and went after Throckmorton.

"Darkness doesn't frighten girls." As Laura passed through the doorway her eyes grew as large as pancakes.

"Who's scared?" Kerry squeaked, and followed.

The room was as dark as chimney soot. It felt damp and cold. The only light came through the leaning door. There were no windows to bring in fresh air.

"This place stinks," said Laura.

"I can't find a door." Kerry felt along the wall.

"Don't move." The strange, deep voice stopped the trio. "I've got a weapon. If you come closer, I'll use it."

Kerry turned and ran for the door with Laura and Charlie pushing him.

Running full speed they raced down the tiny hill and lunged behind a large rock. Throckmorton placed his paws over his eyes.

"Is he coming after us?" Charlie asked Kerry.

"How do I know?"

"Well, look."

"Why me? He might have a gun."

"I'll look," said Laura. "He didn't shoot when we ran, so he must not have a gun."

Ever so carefully, Laura inched her head sideways just enough to show one eye.

"No one's coming."

"On three we'll run for the boat," Charlie ordered. "One—"

"Why?" asked Laura.

"Why what?" said Charlie. "Two—"

"We don't know anything about that man," reasoned Laura.

"That's why we're leaving," said Kerry.

"Not too quickly. What if he's hurt or wounded or crippled. Maybe he needs us," Laura continued.

"You know I'm all for adventure," said Charlie

bravely. "But you don't get close to strangers in dark rooms. Especially if they say they have a weapon."

"I know that, you dense," Laura argued. "But how would you like to read next month that they found the bones of a man on Randolph Island? Then you'd know you killed him."

"I don't want to kill him—I just want to get out of here."

"Then you can't come back and search for treasure, because you're chicken," Laura declared.

"I am not chicken."

"We know, Charlie. You love adventure," Laura continued. "Now let's go to the boat and get a bucket and a couple of oars."

Nervously they gathered their equipment and were soon in front of the old lighthouse. Charlie and Kerry each hoisted an oar.

"Don't worry, Charlie, no one can see in there anyway." Laura pushed the bucket over his head. "If he comes near you, you'll be protected. We'll be right at the door ready to rush in if he tries anything."

Laura turned Charlie toward the door and guided him in. Holding his oar high, he cautiously took each step. When he felt he had walked far enough, Charlie stopped.

"I'm Charlie Dean." His timid voice rang from inside the tin bucket. "My friends are just outside the door. We also have a ferocious dog that can tear people apart. One call from me, one word from me, and he will attack."

Charlie waited for a reply, a sound—anything. Not one word came. Maybe the man had left, Charlie hoped. Or maybe he was sneaking up behind him, Charlie feared.

"If you're thinking of rushing me, forget it." Charlie backed up, tempted to run. "I took second place in the 120-pound class at the school wrestling tournament." He felt right away that he had made a mistake in giving his weight away.

"Ask him if he's hurt," called Laura.

"Are you hurt? Can we help you?"

Scratch. Charlie swung in the direction of the sound. It was a match striking across the concrete floor. Charlie saw the light flicker on the floor.

"Don't move," said the deep voice. "Remember, I have a weapon. What is your name?"

"I'm Chesapeake Charlie—u-u-h—that is Charlie Dean. And I have two strong, armed friends just outside the door."

"Take your bucket off."

Charlie felt a slight panic run through his body. What was the man up to? Why had he listened to Laura? He wished he were in that boat rowing away.

"Don't forget my friends," he said as he put his oar down and reached for his tin helmet. "Now let me see you."

The man moved into the glow of the candle. He was a black man dressed in a blue sea jacket.

"Call me Andrew. Bring your friends in."

Laura and Kerry heard the invitation and moved cautiously into the dark room. Throckmorton followed but remained behind Laura.

"Why are you here?" asked Charlie. "Are you hurt?"

"Do you live here?" asked Laura.

"Maybe he's a murderer," Kerry blurted out.

"Shhh," Charlie hissed while Laura grabbed Kerry.

"I don't blame you for being afraid, but I won't harm you. I have been here for two days and have had nothing to eat."

"How did you get here?" Charlie noticed the accent in the man's speech.

"I have to trust you; but remember, if you tell anyone, my life may be in danger."

"You can trust us, Mr. Andrew," Kerry volunteered.

"Andrew isn't my real name, but it's easier for you to pronounce. I come from Solona off the African coast. Our leader is a ruthless dictator. When he ordered all teachers arrested, I had to find a way out. So I joined the crew of a ship. When they anchored in the Chesapeake Bay, I climbed over the side and swam for land. That was two days ago. I just barely made it to this island. I was exhausted from the swim and am now terribly hungry."

"No problem Andrew, or whatever your name is. We have a boat and can take you straight to shore," Charlie said.

"No," Andrew objected. "The ship I left is still in the Bay. The crew will be looking for me to take me back, and that means prison. I must stay hidden until the ship leaves."

"But we'll take you to the police," Charlie suggested.

"It isn't that simple. If the crew hears about it, the police may be forced to surrender me. After the ship leaves I will gladly go to the authorities."

"How long can that be?" Laura asked.

"Probably just a couple of days. But if they are de-termined to find me, it could be longer."

"Then we have to help," declared Laura.

"No doubt about it," Charlie agreed. "We can bring you food, and blankets for the night. You can count on us keeping your secret. But you have to keep ours, too."

"What is that?" he asked.

"We're hot on the trail of Blackbeard's treasure," Charlie said proudly. "We have a real map and every-thing."

"Your secret is safe with me," Andrew smiled.

"What's the name of the ship?" Laura asked.

"It's the *Whirlwind*. Don't get near it, but if you find out anything, let me know."

"Count on us, Andrew," Charlie told him. "We have some strawberries and cookies left in the boat. We'll get them for you and then head back to get you some real food."

"But remember," Andrew warned, "these men are extremely dangerous. Don't get yourselves hurt."

"No need to worry. We have our bucket and oars."

Andrew grinned widely.

The three went running out.

"Laura and I will get the shovels and detector. Kerry, you run down and get the food."

"Maybe not," said Kerry, as he stopped running.

"Okay," said Charlie. "You get the shovels. I'll get the food."

"Maybe not," he repeated.

"What's wrong with you?" asked Laura.

"Nothing, I just don't want to be part of this."

"Are you kidding?" Charlie asked.

"Don't tell me you're chicken," ventured Laura.

"You can't call me chicken. I let alligators loose with Charlie. It's just—well, not this one."

"We have no time to play guessing games, Kerry. What's wrong?" Charlie yelled.

"Well, it's—it's—"

"Spit it out," Laura demanded.

"He's black."

"He's what?"

"That's it. He's black."

"What in the world has that got to do with anything?" asked Charlie, bewildered.

"My Uncle Ben says you can't trust blacks."

"You're nuts," Laura blurted out.

"He says there are already too many blacks in this country."

"Kerry, I can't believe this. You go to school with blacks every day—and Mexicans and that one Chinese boy."

"I'll get my uncle to explain it to you. You help Andrew if you want. I'll just stay here and dig for the treasure."

"I don't have time to argue." Charlie sounded frustrated. "You dig. We'll go. It will take us hours, but I'll try and get the motorboat this time."

Laura and Charlie ran to the shoreline.

"Wait a minute," said Charlie. "We don't have any time to lose. We'll have to give my speedboat trick a try."

"Speedboat trick?" Laura said sarcastically.

"This is an emergency, Laura, so just do as you're told. Gather large rocks and put them in the back of the boat. We don't have a motor, but we can do the next best thing."

Obediently, Laura began to gather rocks while Charlie stacked them under the back seat.

"How many more do you need?"

"Plenty. Probably five if they're big enough."

"Shouldn't we put the boat in the water first?"

"That's why guys are smarter than girls. A girl would carry each rock to the water. A guy knows enough to put the rocks in the boat and then pull it down to the water." Charlie pointed to his temple.

"Have you ever done this before?" asked Laura.

"Nope. I've been saving this plan for an emergency."

Finally the rear of the boat was loaded and the two began to pull. The boat sank deeply into the sand and they could barely budge it. After several minutes of hard tugging, they arrived at the shore. Charlie sat down on the side of the boat breathing heavily.

"That was really stupid," gasped Laura.

Charlie just pointed at his head, unable to talk.

When the boat entered the water, its bow rose slightly and its stern sank deeply.

"Climb in," said Charlie.

"It'll sink," warned Laura.

"Never. With the bow raised, there is less friction. We will be the fastest rowboat in the Bay."

The vessel moved slowly, the top of its bow only two inches out of the water.

"Stroke, stroke, stroke," commanded Charlie.

"Any minute now we'll drown," moaned Laura.

"Stroke, stroke, stroke."

Chapter Four

Breathing heavily, Laura and Charlie could barely drag themselves out of the boat.

" 'Put rocks in the boat.' Charlie Dean, you have rocks in your head!" Laura said, still panting.

"I know it was harder." Charlie could hardly talk. "But you'd be surprised how much faster it was."

"Faster nothing! Where did you dream up this clunky idea?" Her breathing sounded like a steam engine.

Charlie merely pointed at his temple, and they began to trudge slowly toward the house.

"Thanks for letting us eat over at the island," said Charlie as he stuffed sandwiches into his sack.

"That's fine, but I still can't see you three eating twelve sandwiches and two large bags of potato chips. Be sure and bring back any of those pickles you don't eat."

"And we need three quarts of soda," Charlie declared.

"Three quarts—for three people?" Mrs. Dean was startled. "What are you going to do, open a refreshment stand?"

"Just this once, Mom. It'll be all right."

"Are you sure you want these fried oysters on top of that?"

The aroma of oysters frying in the pan always made Charlie hungrier than a goat. He had to move away from the stove to stop his mouth from watering.

"Those six will be fine," Charlie said as he picked up the box of food.

"Laura, bring the soda and oysters, and grab that bag I brought from the basement." He moved out the back door.

"Tell him to be careful, Laura," Mrs. Dean warned. "When I was grocery shopping this morning there were two African men in the store showing a picture to everyone. They're looking for someone, and they said he may be crazy. Seems he got confused and left their ship. They want to find him and take him back to his family. Well, anyway, be careful."

Laura ran out back with the freshly wrapped oysters and soda bottles in her arms.

"We'd better get moving," she told Charlie. "I'll explain later."

This time Charlie took the boat with the outboard motor.

The craft roared swiftly toward the island. Laura sat close to Charlie and by shouting explained what Mrs. Dean had told her.

"Does Andrew seem crazy to you?" Charlie asked.

"Well, how would I know? We need to talk to him some more."

"It sounds like a lie to me," said Charlie. "But we'll check him out."

The trip took only 20 minutes with the motor wide open. The sun was starting to go down and clouds were beginning to glide across the sky.

Charlie and Laura struggled to the top of the

island, their arms loaded with provisions. "Let's find Kerry first," Charlie suggested.

They walked over to the tree where Kerry had been digging. "Kerry, Kerry," they called. He didn't answer.

A glance into the hole sent alarm ringing through their brains. There were Kerry's shirt and shoes. Laura jumped into the hole and picked up the shirt.

"There's something red on the sleeve." Laura handed the garment to Charlie.

"It looks like blood," Charlie concluded.

"You don't think. . ." Laura began to climb up out of the hole. They stood together not knowing what to say.

"Kerry!" Laura called.

"Shhhh!" cautioned Charlie. "We better keep quiet until we find out what's happened. Where's Throckmorton? You'd at least think he'd come running."

"Maybe Andrew *is* crazy." Laura said softly.

"No. There's an explanation for all of this. I just wish I knew what it was. We'd better stick together."

"Should we go back to the boat?" Laura wondered. "What if Andrew gets our boat? Then we have no way off this island."

"We'll have to take that chance. We need to make sure Kerry's safe. I don't see either shovel. Kerry couldn't be using both of them."

"Then maybe, just maybe," Laura spoke haltingly, "Andrew has both shovels and can use them for weapons."

"Poor Throckmorton."

"You mean, 'Poor Kerry,' " said Laura.

"Yeah, I suppose I'd miss him, too."

"Let's tear some branches off this bush. At least we can camouflage ourselves." Laura began to pull on the tall twigs.

Each of them was able to tear loose a branch to match their height. Holding them up as shields they tiptoed around the island. Every time the breeze hit the tall grass, Laura and Charlie quivered with fright.

"Thump, thump."

"Shhh!" Charlie grabbed Laura. "What's that noise?"

"I don't know."

"It's over by that dead tree." Charlie nodded in the direction of an old twisted trunk.

"Sounds like someone is digging a—"

"Don't say it," said Charlie. "We don't know what it is. You stay here. I'll crawl up and see who it is."

Charlie started toward the trunk while Laura stood behind her branch. She wished she had gone with Charlie. In a minute Charlie came racing back, breathless.

"Charlie, you're white as a ghost!"

"It's Andrew! Andrew's digging, and there's no Throckmorton—I mean Kerry."

"We can't leave," said Laura. "We'll have to jump Andrew and find out what happened."

"Are your knees shaking?" Charlie asked.

"Try not to think about it." Laura attempted to shrug it off. "We have to do what we have to do."

"Thump, thump."

The sounds of digging grew louder as the two edged closer to the old tree. Their branches were held high. Andrew didn't look up when the duo reached the tree. He was already waist deep in the hole.

Charlie and Laura perched, ready to leap on their victim.

"Yeeh!" A shrieking voice made both of them jump and whirl around.

It was Kerry standing behind them. He was shoeless, shirtless, and carrying a stick like a tribal warrior.

"You bonehead!" shouted Charlie.

"Didn't scare you, did I?"

"Of course not," answered Laura as she straightened her shirt and tried to look calm.

"That was Kerry's idea." Andrew peeked around the trunk. "I told him I would just as soon keep digging and let him sneak up on you."

"But where's Throckmorton?" asked Charlie.

"Last time I saw him he was asleep by the lighthouse."

"How did the blood get on your shirt?" Laura wanted to know.

"That was nothing. I picked up a broken bottle and cut my hand—no big deal. It's stopped bleeding. Did you think I was hurt or something?"

"Of course not." Laura turned her head and walked away.

"We brought some food along," said Charlie.

In a few minutes all four were near the lighthouse and had laid out their food on an old green blanket. Throckmorton was busy begging from everyone. Charlie tossed him a sandwich.

"How did you talk Andrew into helping you dig, Kerry?" asked Laura.

"He didn't have to. I was so tired of hiding in this

dark lighthouse that I *asked* him to let me dig."

"I can't believe it," said Charlie.

"Well, Kerry couldn't either at first, but we had a long talk. Nothing helps conversation like two men working together."

"I told Andrew about some of the things my uncle said to me. It wasn't anything he hadn't heard before."

"There are bigots all over the world," Andrew added, "who hate people because of their color, or their size, or their nationality. If I were not a Christian, it would probably bother me even more than it does."

"You're a Christian?" asked Charlie.

"Yes, and there are still people I don't care for, but I'm working on it. Jesus would not have disliked a person because of his skin."

"Is there prejudice in Africa?" asked Laura.

"Much," Andrew laughed. "One tribe doesn't like another. Some blacks dislike Orientals, and some whites dislike everybody. But fortunately there are also some who love others, no matter what. That's what gives us hope."

"Pass the oysters," said Kerry.

"Did Laura tell you about the two men?" asked Charlie.

"Yes, and that doesn't surprise me. They won't give up easily."

"May I have some chips?" Kerry pleaded.

"For the next few days you had better stay low," advised Charlie. "We need to go back home tonight, but we'll come first thing in the morning. We'll check to see what we can find out about those men."

"That's another place where your uncle misunderstands, Kerry. He said black people are lazy. Wait until you see how hard those men search for me."

"My uncle said it; I didn't."

"I realize that," said Andrew. "But do me a favor and tell him the Africans built Timbuktu—a thousand years before New York City or Boston. And it was a fully developed civilization."

"I'll tell him."

"My Bible tells me there is no free or slave, or male or female, no Jews or Greeks. In Jesus Christ we are the same."

"I knew you weren't crazy," Laura blurted out.

"Thanks. I had a feeling you weren't either," laughed Andrew.

"We have to go back," Charlie explained. "But we won't leave you without protection. Laura, hand me that bag. Where's Throckmorton?"

Throckmorton came trotting around the corner. Charlie petted his neck and ruffled his ears.

"We really need you, old boy. This is going to take some good acting, but you can do it. Get that bag," Charlie ordered Laura. "Now stand still."

Charlie opened the bag and pulled out his tiger rug.

"This might make you feel funny at first, but it's for a good cause. Be still."

He laid the rug across Throckmorton's back and stretched its legs down to match the beagle's. Removing string from the bag, he began to tie the rug on his legs. One long string went around his back to hold it firmly in place. The head piece flapped up and Charlie tied string loosely around his neck.

"There," Charlie announced. "Now if you could

just growl like a tiger. If any boat comes near the island, they may see Tiger-Morton and decide to sail away. It's a long shot but it can't hurt. And we'll bring you some water and dogfood in the morning, too."

"At least he makes good company," Andrew agreed as he patted his newly constructed tiger.

"We have to go," said Charlie.

Charlie, Laura, and Kerry started toward their boat.

"So Tiger-Morton was your idea," said Laura sourly. "When the squirrels come out, you'd better keep your brain in a cage."

"You just wish you'd thought of it!" snapped Charlie.

"Listen, if I had thought of that dud, I'd sell my brain for bean-bag stuffing."

"Jealous!" chirped Charlie.

As they rode away in the motorboat, they looked back to see an African waving to them, standing next to the oddest tiger man has ever seen.

The next morning as the sun rose, Laura and Kerry were at Charlie's house. They were excited to help Andrew.

"We can't go back to the island until we find out what's happening with those guys who are looking for Andrew," said Charlie. "My mom said there were two men at the door yesterday looking for him."

"They came to my house, too," Laura added. "Evidently they're combing the neighborhood."

"But no one can help them," Kerry assured. "We're the only ones who know where he is."

"I bet it wouldn't take long to find the men and

make sure they don't start searching islands," Charlie thought out loud. "Maybe we could even set up a little runaround for them."

"What is your evil mind thinking, Charlie Dean?" asked Laura.

"It's really simple. Kerry, they haven't been to your house yet. If you managed to answer the door, you could get this plot started."

"Knock, knock." It was a firm, loud rap on Kerry's door.

"We're looking for this man." They pushed a picture toward Kerry. "He is very sick, but he left a ship near here. We need to find him and return him to his relatives. Have you seen him?"

"I don't think so, but let me look closer. You say he left a ship?"

"Yes. The poor man isn't in his right mind. We just hope we can find him before he hurts himself or someone else."

"Hmmm. I can't be sure."

"Think hard, it's important."

"Well, this may not be him, of course, but I saw someone who looked like him eating at the Pizzarama in town. Maybe someone there can help you. It's in the Cloverleaf Shopping Center."

Hurrying toward the car, neither man paused to say thank you.

"Have you seen this man?" the taller one asked the manager.

"Well, I haven't," he answered, "but let me ask our waitress. Stella, Stella. These gentlemen are looking for this man. Have you seen him?"

"Well, I'm not sure. Let me see." Laura was wearing a waitress uniform and a hat pulled down to her ears.

"Maybe you can see the picture better if you take your sunglasses off. How can you see in here?"

"Can't do that," she insisted. "My eyes are sensitive to the candles on the tables. I can see all right. This man does look familiar. Sure, he was in here yesterday."

"Do you know where he went?"

"Why are you so interested?"

"We—we have good news for him. He has won a prize and we need to give it to him. It's a lot of money."

"I wouldn't know where he went, but he did ask me where the skating rink was."

"The skating rink?"

"Yes. That's right. He said he always wanted to skate. It's on the other side of town on Douglas Street. I believe it's open today."

When the men arrived at the rink, they saw a boy sitting by the door with a pair of skates in his hand. Pete tried to look cool. As they approached, Pete stood up and moved toward the entrance.

"Hey, boy. Have you seen this man?"

"Oh, sure. I talked to him for about an hour yesterday." The second he said it Pete walked through the entrance and disappeared.

"Hey! Wait a minute!" They followed him inside.

"Hold it." The manager was standing by the door. "You can't come in without a ticket."

"How much?" the shorter one asked impatiently.

"A buck-fifty each. Plus you'll need skates."

"We don't want to skate," the tall one explained.

"Sorry, no one can come in without skates."

"How much?" The shorter one answered impatiently.

"Another seventy-five cents each."

"Okay."

"What size?"

"What size what?"

"What size *skates?*"

The men were finally inside, each holding a pair of black skates and looking around. Pete was at the far side of the rink skating backwards. Other skaters whizzed past him.

"There he is," said the short one, trotting toward the rink.

"Hold it!" A man with a whistle on his neck skated up to the gate. "No one gets on the floor without skates. You'll have to put them on."

"Listen, fella, how would you like to—"

"Quiet," said the short one. "We don't want trouble. Of course, we'll put the skates on."

They sat down on a bench and took off their shoes.

"Can you skate?" asked the tall one.

"No, but how hard can it be?"

"Some of them are moving pretty fast." He pulled on his first skate.

"We will just go slowly."

The men launched out onto the rink like robots with several transistors missing. Each had his legs spread in a desperate attempt to stay up. Arms outstretched, legs stiff, they more sailed than skated. The men watched their feet with riveted attention. The tall one looked up; he yelled and threw his arms across his face. A dozen skaters came rushing toward them. The short one crouched low and wrapped his arms around his head. The tall one was brushed by a skater and went into a spin. He twirled around three times and then his left leg shot out, sending him crashing to the floor.

"You two had better turn around," someone warned them. "You're going in the wrong direction."

They nodded but didn't answer.

"Take my hand," the tall one told the short one. As he rose halfway up, the short one lost his balance and went flying against his partner. Both collapsed in a heap of legs, arms and banging skates. Another herd of skaters whisked past them.

After considerable struggling, both men reached a position where they could barely shuffle around the rink. The shorter man remained in a crouch and moved by pushing his hands on the floor. The taller man stood erect and hugged the walls. Each movement was dangerous as he tried to find a ledge to hold onto.

Meanwhile, Pete was skating figure eights and staying on the far side of the rink.

After some agonizing effort the two men finally reached Pete. His enormous smile suggested he was having a better time than his two visitors.

"You guys skated much?" Pete joked.

"Have you seen this man?" the tall one glided toward Pete.

"I told you I have. Let me show you how to do a circle." He grabbed an extended arm and whipped him around.

"Aaah," groaned the tall man as he spread his legs and began to go helplessly in a circle.

"Relax!" shouted young Pete. "Relax!"

The shorter man had managed to scoot over toward Pete. Pete shot behind the man and thrust his hands under the man's arms, lifting him straight up.

"You'll never be able to skate crouched down." As he picked the man up he also pushed him briskly.

"Aaah!" He went sailing for ten feet and plunk. He hit the floor like a suitcase full of bricks.

The tall man stopped beside his fallen friend. He awkwardly helped him to his feet and they struggled toward Pete, locked nervously in each other's arm.

"Let's try a whip," Pete said as he rushed to their side. He jerked at the tall man's free arm and began to pull. With his friend holding on for his life they whirled around. Pete was picking up speed as he pulled. After three fast, full turns he let go. The two men took off rapidly toward the side of the rink. Boom! They smashed into the guard rail and collapsed on the floor.

Pete skated over to them.

"That's enough lessons for one day," he announced. "About that picture, that man was here yesterday. He said he wanted to rent a boat and go to an island. I sent him over to Clyde at Biff's Wharf. That's all I know."

Abruptly, Pete turned and skated away.

Chapter Five

Charlie watched the two men walking down the pier. The tall man moved stiffly as if his back ached. A severe limp made the short man waddle.

Nervously, Charlie pulled up the collar on his raincoat and tugged his cap down tighter.

"Are you Clyde?" they asked.

"That's me." Charlie tried to sound gruff.

"We hear you took this man to an island yesterday." They handed him the picture.

"Looks familiar."

"It was only yesterday," the tall one reminded him.

"That's right," Charlie replied slowly. "That's right. He wanted to go to Deeron Island. Nice man, really friendly."

"Did you bring him back?"

"Nope. He wanted to stay. Mrs. Schultz runs a boarding house. I suppose he spent the night there."

"Can you run us over there?"

"Depends."

"On what?" asked the shorter one.

"Depends on whether or not each of you has five dollars."

"You've got it." The tall man handed Charlie a ten.

"Ouch," said the short man as he climbed into the boat.

"Your leg looks like it's out of shape. Has it been that way long?" asked Charlie.

"Just happened today. Never mind, let's go."

Charlie started his engine and the boat purred out onto the Bay.

"Do you always wear that raincoat?" asked the tall man. "It must get hot."

"You never know," said Charlie. "Storms come up quickly on the Bay."

The trio was quiet for the rest of the trip. Fifteen minutes later they arrived at Deeron Island. Mrs. Schultz's Boarding House was a large blue building on Main street.

Laughter rolled across Charlie's backyard as the quartet retold their stories.

"So he asked, 'Couldn't you see better without your sunglasses?' " said Laura, and they laughed again.

"I don't know what you did to them, Pete, but when I saw them they sure walked funny," kidded Charlie. "This will waste a full day for them. They can't get off Deeron Island until tomorrow morning when the ferryboat goes over there."

"Each day is important to Andrew," added Kerry.

"Mom won't let us leave for another hour," said Charlie, "so we can get some jobs done."

"There's no reason to hurry," said Laura sarcastically. "Tiger-beagle is there to protect Andrew." She was sitting on the ground between Charlie and Kerry who were on the bench. Pete was lying on the picnic table.

"You're jealous, Laura," Charlie insisted. Whether or not you like it, boys are much smarter than girls."

"Here goes that trash again," Laura moaned.

"I'm afraid Charlie is correct again." Kerry chimed.

"I guess that explains why girls receive most of the school honors," Laura said in frustration.

"That's simple book work." Kerry refused to yield. "Anybody can memorize and repeat it back."

"Spell 'procrastination,' " Laura ordered.

"A perfect example," said Kerry. "Spelling is a non-skill. People who *spell* become secretaries. People who *think* become executives."

"What is pi-squared times 160?" Laura was irritated.

"That's not even important. The only pi-squaring you will ever do is in the kitchen. My uncle says that's where women belong. They're happiest there. Take them outside and they only start trouble."

"Is this some kind of joke?" she asked.

"Not at all. Why do you see so few women doctors and lawyers and professors? There are only a handful of women in top business jobs. It's the law of natural superiority. Those who have it rise to the top. Those who don't settle into the home."

"So women become mothers because they aren't as good as men?" she asked.

"I didn't want to put it that bluntly, but those are the facts. My uncle calls it 'creative conquests.' "

"Then why does the Constitution say all people are created equal?" Laura asked calmly.

"It says 'men,' Laura; it says *men* are created equal."

Charlie and Pete began to snicker as they watched the two argue.

"Don't get me wrong, Laura. I don't have anything against women. They are just dependent on the stronger, brighter male."

"Arguing won't prove anything," Laura announced as she sprang up from the ground. "Let's put it to the test."

"You mean that spelling and pi-squaring stuff?" he mocked.

"No, no. A real *man* contest. Let's run one lap around the yard. You give me a little head start, and since you are better, you won't have any trouble catching me."

"How much head start?"

"Just ten feet. Here, I'll move back a little. That's it. Just this much."

"Don't stand up." Charlie's hand pushed the rising Kerry back onto the bench. "You can beat her from a sitting start."

"Sure," said Kerry.

"Sure," said Charlie.

"Sure," said Laura. "You start us, Pete."

"Ready."

Laura crouched down for a fast start.

"Get set."

Kerry leaned forward on the bench.

"Go!" Pete shouted.

Laura darted forward. Kerry rose from the bench and took an awkward jerk forward. His feet twisted and his body spun.

"Hey!" he yelled and collapsed into an ugly heap on the ground. His feet couldn't move because his shoestrings had been tied together.

Charlie roared with laughter and Pete bent over in hysterics. Laura stopped running and rolled on the ground laughing uncontrollably.

"You're a sneaky rat, Laura!" Kerry shouted. "Only an inferior person would do that."

"It looked like" . . . she could barely talk . . . "it looked like a creative conquest to me!"

After the four pulled themselves back together again, Charlie made them get serious.

"Where does your uncle get all those crazy ideas?" Charlie asked Kerry.

"They aren't so crazy." Kerry was trying to untie his shoes.

"Why, sure they are," said Laura. "Especially his notions about black people."

"Andrew may be different, but blacks and whites usually aren't the same," Kerry continued.

"But how are they different?" Charlie asked.

"Don't get me wrong. Like I said, Andrew is all right. But you don't see black people going into white churches, or white people into black churches. We just *know* we're different," Kerry tried to explain.

"It's not because we're different," said Laura.

"Well, then why?" asked Kerry. "Why don't blacks and whites go to the same churches?"

"It's because—well—I don't know," Charlie stuttered. "I guess they just like their ways and we like ours."

"That sounds lame," added Laura. "We have the same God, don't we?"

"Sure," said Charlie.

"And many blacks and whites believe in Jesus,

don't they?" she asked.

"Sure, but—" Charlie mumbled.

"But what?" Laura interrupted. "The plain fact is that many of us are just prejudiced. We don't like people who are different. It's the same reason Kerry thinks girls aren't as good as boys. We are just different."

"My uncle's the one who said it," Kerry insisted.

"Yes, but you believe it, too," Charlie said.

"Well—maybe I half-believe it," Kerry admitted begrudgingly.

"It's all a bunch of junk," Charlie commented. "Look at Dave Banks. He's black and gets almost all A's. And you couldn't meet a nicer guy. And Gwen Davis—you couldn't meet a better Christian. So what's the difference?"

"I don't know," said Kerry, feeling a bit cornered. "But my uncle insists there is a difference."

"And a bad difference at that?" Laura asked.

"I suppose. But not Andrew. Wait till you get to know him. He's terrific," Kerry concluded.

"My dad has a favorite verse he quotes all the time," Charlie volunteered. "It's from some place in First John. It says, 'If we can't love our brother whom we can see, how can we love God whom we can't see?' or something like that. I suppose that means blacks, whites, and all kinds."

"I think things are better than they used to be," said Laura. "There was sure a lot of racial trouble here in the sixties. People still talk about the trouble at Cambridge."

"Things are a lot better," Charlie agreed, "but it's still tough. The paper says there were 29 cross burnings by the KKK last year in Maryland. That's terrible."

"That isn't Christian," said Kerry.

"Not by a long shot," Charlie continued. "Many Christian blacks and whites are getting along great, but that doesn't mean we all are."

"And women?" Laura stared Kerry in the eyes.

"If they're all like you—they must be weird," Kerry said.

"Let's knock it off," Charlie ordered. "If we spend all day trying to straighten you two out, we'll never get any food out to Andrew. Besides, all he has for company is Throckmorton."

"You mean Tiger-beagle," joked Laura.

The quartet was soon in the house and garage, cleaning out the refrigerator, freezer, and pantry. Cans, bags, loaves, soda, and a sack of charcoal were soon flying into boxes. Young legs hurried the cargo out to the motorboat by the pier. As they moved through the yard, they all picked up any tool they could imagine using. Crab nets, buckets, a hatchet, a hunting knife all went hurling into the vessel.

When they had reassembled inside the house, Charlie again took charge. "My mom should be home any minute and then we can take off. Kerry and I will spend the night while Laura and Pete come home."

"Why me?" Pete whined.

"It has to be someone." Charlie continued, "You two can come back and pick up any news about those two guys and the *Whirlwind*."

"No fun," Pete groaned.

"There is one thing we don't want to forget and that's the reason why we went to Randolph Island in the first place," said Charlie.

"Blackbeard's treasure!" Kerry blurted out.

"Exactly." Charlie explained, "Naturally, Andrew is more important than the gold, but we certainly aren't forgetting it."

"Twenty lousy percent," Laura complained.

"It might not be a bad idea to write the Bay Marine Historical Society. They might be able to tell us if they know anything about a Blackbeard's treasure on Randolph Island," said Charlie. "I've got it! If I send them a Chesapeake Charlie speed-o-card we should hear from them in a few days."

"I'm afraid to ask what a Chesapeake Charlie speed-o-card is," said Laura.

"I'll show you, but I don't ever want any of you using one."

Without waiting for a reaction, Charlie walked over to the writing desk in the hall and pulled out a large round cardboard.

"I got these from the Pizzarama for a nickel apiece. When I want a quick reply I use these for postcards. They won't get lost in the mail and secretaries can't ignore them."

"What is it?" asked Kerry. "Maybe a foot and a half across?"

"But it doesn't weigh anything so I can send one for 41 cents, first class."

"The post office takes them?" asked a disbelieving Laura.

"The first time I did it they frowned and scratched their heads a lot, but now they just smile. It's a lot cheaper than a telegram."

Charlie took a dark felt-tip pen and wrote his note

in large letters. He then copied the address of the Bay Marine Historical Society from the phone book.

"Nothing to it," he said proudly.

"Pizza cards and tiger-beagles," groaned Laura in disgust, "and Kerry thinks boys are smarter than girls. What is this world coming to?"

"We have to get going as soon as my mother gets here," said Charlie. "Where's Pete? Somebody find Pete."

The trio scouted around the yard but couldn't find Charlie's brother. They called and yelled but received no reply.

"Let's leave without the clown," Kerry said impatiently.

"No, you check behind the shed and I'll look in the basement," Charlie said as he started toward the house.

"Hey, hey," Laura was whispering as loud as she could. "Over here."

Kerry and Charlie ran to her as she motioned for them to keep quiet.

"What's wrong?" asked Charlie.

"Shhh! I found Pete behind those trees, but don't make any noise."

As they tiptoed toward the wide maple trees, they smelled a strong, coarse odor.

"What's that?" Kerry wrinkled his nose.

"He must be burning incense," said Charlie.

"I don't think so," Laura said with a silly grin.

"Looks like smoke," Kerry mouthed the words almost without a sound.

"Cough, cough." A choking sound came from behind the trees.

The noise became louder and the smoke rose in large, dark puffs.

The trio slithered behind a stump only ten feet from Pete. They could see him clearly, but he didn't notice his audience. Even if he had wanted to see them, the smoke would have made it impossible for his eyes to focus.

"What's he doing?" asked Kerry.

No one answered as Pete held a long, brown paper tube to his mouth and inhaled deeply. His eyes grew huge as smoke poured from his lips and covered his face.

"He's smoking paper bags," Charlie whispered.

"Paper bags?" said Kerry.

"Didn't you ever do that?" Charlie asked. "It'll make you sicker than a dog."

"Let's surprise him." Kerry started to rise.

"No," commanded Laura. "Lets see how far this dodo goes."

Pete inhaled as deeply as he could and each time the smoke covered his face like an old steam engine. He hacked, coughed and spit. But no sooner had he cleared his throat than Pete sucked in another load.

"We'd better say something," said Kerry. "The idiot's going to kill himself."

"It's too much fun watching him get sick," noted Laura.

Refusing to budge, the three of them watched the boy continue his self-torture. They noticed that he was slowing down. In between puffs he would merely sit and stare into space. Finally, Pete would drag again on the paper furnace. He inhaled so hard, fire rose up on the end of the paper and smoke practically covered his head.

After five or ten long minutes Pete slowly crushed his homemade cigar on a rock next to him. As he pushed it down he missed the rock as often as he hit it.

Without a sound Pete lay on his left side almost facing his onlookers. The color in his face had become chalk white. Pete's eyes looked like pools of pea soup.

"Augh, augh." With no more sound than that, Pete's stomach wrenched and he threw up. Too sick to move, he lay in the same position for a couple of minutes and then threw up again.

"Now let's surprise him," said the anxious Kerry.

"No," said Charlie. "Let's let him suffer in peace. Later we can find a good time to mention it."

Laura agreed and the three of them silently made their way back toward the house.

Charlie's mother soon arrived home and gave the group final permission to leave. They carried a few more supplies to the motorboat and prepared to depart.

"This time let's forget about the special speedboat," Laura snapped.

"What special speedboat?" asked Kerry.

"Never mind," said Charlie crisply.

"The one with the rocks," Laura continued.

"Rocks?" asked Kerry.

"Forget it," Charlie shouted. "It isn't my fault Laura's afraid to try new things."

As they dumped the last box into the boat, a staggering figure came waddling toward them. Pete still didn't look his best.

"Hey, Pete," Kerry shouted, "where have you been?"

"Boy, you don't look so hot," said Laura, barely

holding back her laughter.

"I just don't feel too good," said Pete lifelessly.

"You can tell us about it," continued Laura.

"Yeah," said Charlie, "we won't let it out of the *bag*."

The trio burst into uncontrollable laughter. Pete was puzzled but decided to remain silent just in case they didn't know.

They launched off with Charlie at the motor, Laura sitting in the bow, and Kerry and Pete in the middle. Each wore a life jacket. Charlie knew he would get grounded for driving the motorboat without preservers.

"They're clamming!" shouted Charlie as he nodded toward the boat a few hundred yards away. "Picking up those delicious mano clams."

"Is it sinking?" asked Kerry.

"No, it always lists to the starboard because of the huge motors."

"Why?" Kerry wondered.

"To pick up the clams. It has a giant vacuum cleaner that sucks up everything on the bottom of the Bay. It sucks it onto a giant treadmill that carries the clams and everything else up to the boat."

"Sounds tough on the poor Bay," Laura joined in.

"Some people think it's too tough. That's why the government limits clamming. Just so much a day, and in certain areas."

"What do they do with all the gook they bring up?" Laura asked.

"Everything gets dropped back except the legal clams. Even the little ones are dumped. There isn't much of a market for 'gook.' " Charlie laughed.

The boat sliced smoothly through the water, and the first half of the short trip went quickly. The three were then surprised by Charlie's sudden announcement.

"Look at those clouds." He pointed across to a fast-moving system above the Bay. The top of the clouds was cottony white, but the bottom was dark.

"It's getting cold," complained Laura.

"I'm afraid it will hit us before we reach land," said Charlie.

Crack! Lightning sliced through the clouds and frightened everyone.

"Hold on and we'll try to make it." Charlie pulled the collar closed on his shirt and lowered his head. A few cold drops began to fall on their bare heads and arms.

"There's Randolph." Laura pointed to the small island ahead of them. The rain became heavier.

"We can't make it," said Charlie. "So hold tight."

The waters became rougher and began to chop in little sharp waves. Rain started to sweep over them in a steady downpour soaking everyone.

"I've got to cut the engine," Charlie yelled. "We're hitting the waves too hard. We'll just have to float."

Pete had pulled his shirt tail over his back and onto his head. He shivered as the cold rain pelted his bare skin. Kerry had put a metal bucket over his head, making the rain drops sound like shots from a .22 rifle. Laura was holding a flat paper bag to keep herself dry, but it was really useless. The rain drenched all four without the slightest relief.

The bow of the boat jerked sharply into the air and smacked loudly back into the water.

"Keep low," ordered Charlie as he crouched down, one hand on a makeshift umbrella and the other clinging to the side of the boat.

Crack, crack. The lightning snapped like a whip. Each time it cut through the air, they trembled and shrank further into the boat.

The storm passed almost as quickly as it began. The air was still cool and the four shivering bodies raised goose-pimples like hot popcorn. Charlie began yanking at the motor rope to start it again.

As they pulled up to Randolph Island, they were all soaked through to their skin. The bottom of the boat was three inches deep in water, and those who wore socks could feel them squishing in their shoes. Every grocery bag, piece of food, and clothing was drenched.

Laura was the first to step on the shore.

"What bonehead would take us through a thunderstorm?" she growled.

"It came up so quickly," answered Charlie defiantly.

"They don't come *that* quickly." Angrily, she continued, "How can a lug-head be allowed to drive a boat if he doesn't even have enough sense to look at the clouds."

"We were in a hurry," Charlie defended himself. "Besides, I got you here safely, didn't I?"

"My mother sure would be mad if she knew this," said Kerry.

"A lot of credit I get," said Charlie as he pulled the boat farther up on the beach. "I practically saved your lives."

Pete didn't say anything. He bent over by a patch

of tall grass and threw up. Twice!

Andrew was relieved to see his friends had made it back safely. He told them he had watched the clouds form and then swing across the boat. The husky immigrant went right to work gathering wood and starting two fires.

"Laura can use the room in the lighthouse," he explained. "The boys will have to stand by the fire in the field."

"But it's freezing out here," Chesapeake Charlie complained. "Besides, girls are supposed to be tougher than guys."

"No gentleman would hear of forcing a young lady out in the cool breeze," insisted Andrew. "Men consider it a privilege to sacrifice for a woman."

"Ugh," said Kerry.

After Laura disappeared into the lighthouse, each of the boys took off his shirt and socks and began to wring them dry and hang them over a clothesline Andrew had erected.

"We saw two men from the ship," said Charlie.

"I knew they wouldn't give up easily." Andrew looked concerned.

"They have even knocked on doors looking for you," Kerry told him. "But we managed to get rid of them for a while."

"You did?" Andrew's eyes brightened. "How did you do that?"

"Well, first Pete gave them a few first-class skating lessons," Charlie chuckled.

"Then Charlie dropped them off on Deeron Island," said Kerry. "That should keep them busy until tomorrow. By then we'll think of something else."

Pete didn't say anything. He threw up again.

"If I have to hide out someplace," said Andrew, "this is a beautiful spot."

"You really like the Chesapeake Bay, don't you?" Charlie beamed.

"The fresh air is terrific. Plus I can hide behind this tree and watch the fishermen work near the island."

"That can't be done," said Charlie.

"What do you mean?"

"There are no fishermen here. No seamen either. On the Bay they call themselves watermen. It's a strange thing, but they all do that."

"Then watermen it is," Andrew agreed. "It seems like the Chesapeake Bay has a personality all its own—just like Chesapeake Charlie."

"It must bother you being out here alone," said Charlie.

"But I have Throckmorton."

"It has to be scary. You've left your family and your country; you don't know what in the world tomorrow holds."

"Sure, sometimes I get scared, but I can't look back. Besides, it does a lot for my prayer life."

"I bet," Charlie agreed. "It would get me praying."

"I talked to the Lord a lot before I decided to try it. I even asked a couple of my friends to pray with me. In my country you have to be careful whom you ask to pray. You never know who might turn you in. Now I have asked God to help guide me through tomorrow."

Chapter Six

When her clothes were fairly dry, Laura came out to join the others around the fire. The sun had reclaimed the sky, and its warm rays felt good on their damp bodies. Each young person stood as close to the fire as possible.

"There's one thing I still don't understand, Andrew." Charlie's mind was moving. "Why would your government want to arrest teachers?"

"The way they see it," replied Andrew, opening a package of hot dogs, "I'm too open-minded. They only want teachers who believe in their system."

"Well, what's their system?" Charlie continued.

"First, they don't want teachers who believe in God, and if you believe Jesus is the Son of God, they really think you are dangerous."

"Why would a government be afraid of God?" asked Kerry.

"That isn't all. They don't want teachers who believe all people are of equal value," said Andrew.

"What does that mean?" wondered Pete.

"The new government does not trust white men, Orientals, or the darker tribes of people. They consider them inferior and evil. Naturally, I couldn't teach that, so I was considered dangerous."

"I couldn't live in a country like that," said Charlie.

"I hope America isn't that way. But I hear some disturbing stories." Andrew handed everyone a stick and they placed hot dogs on the end.

"Of course not," Charlie blared out. "America is a melting pot."

"Maybe," said Andrew. "It would be impolite of me to discuss this since I am really your guest." He distributed the buns.

"Go ahead," said Laura, "I'm interested."

"Well, I have read some troubling news." Andrew hesitated.

"Like what?" asked Kerry.

"I understand many American Indians are treated badly and live in terrible homes."

"I don't know," Charlie admitted. "I've never met a real Indian."

"I also hear many blacks are looked down on, are poor, and can't get good jobs," Andrew continued. "I even hear that black people are still called names— even by Christians."

"Well—maybe," said Pete. "But I'm sure we don't mean anything by it."

"Sure, but Andrew has a point," said Charlie. "When there are no blacks around, we still sometimes call them niggers."

"But, like Pete says," said Kerry, "we don't mean anything by it."

"Anything that puts another person down is harmful," said Andrew.

"It's just a joke, like a nickname," Kerry insisted.

"Baloney!" Laura interrupted. "It's one thing to kid someone, but it's something else to call him a mean name. No one wants to be called a nigger."

"It's very important to view other people in the

proper light," said Andrew. "If I love you like a brother, I will accept you and won't say mean things. Black people are like Orientals, Indians, and white people. We love, we dream, and many are dedicated to God." Andrew poured a drink and gave a cup to each of the young people.

"But I am very optimistic," Andrew continued. "I think I will enjoy living in America. Someday I hope even to attend church with some of you."

"You won't find many black people in white churches," said Charlie. "And you won't find many white people in black churches either."

"When I read the Bible I see all sorts of people following Jesus Christ," Andrew replied, with concern. "Peter had a Galilean accent that sounded funny to the people in Judea. Jesus also had a friend called Simon the Leper. How would you like to be 'Charlie the Measled,' or 'Pete the Cancered,' or 'Kerry the Diseased'? Jesus collected people of all flavors and colors."

"Like Mary Magdalene!" Laura joined in. "The Bible calls her a sinner. That sounds pretty terrible to me."

"Jesus didn't sift them out and say, 'I only want the nice, neat, clean people to follow me,' " Andrew added.

"That sounds good," said Charlie thoughtfully. "But really, it doesn't make sense to hang around with people who are messy and live in dumps. We can talk about it but it doesn't really work."

"What comes to mind when you think of a beggar?" asked Andrew. "Where I come from they are dirty, have raggedy clothes, and as often as not have bugs crawling on them. Jesus seemed to attract people like that.''

"I never thought of it that way," Kerry admitted.

"Most of us don't, but I think real Christians can treat people who are different as if they were brothers," said Andrew.

"Life would be easier if we were all ghost crabs," Charlie inserted.

"Never heard of one," Andrew replied.

"I think you are about to," Laura said with a groan.

"They are the same color as the sand. If the sun is up all you can see is a shadow running across the beach, but no crab. That way they all look alike."

"Thanks," Andrew laughed. "But I think I'll settle for being a person."

"Has anyone seen Throckmorton?" Pete asked.

"Not since we got back," answered Laura.

"Maybe we should try and find that mutt," said Charlie. "The island isn't that big."

All five fanned out, hot dogs and drinks in their hands, and started to search for the beagle.

"Maybe we should carry chains and whips for that ferocious tiger," Laura warned.

"Ha—ha," replied Charlie sarcastically. "Just wait and see. That disguise might come in pretty handy."

The search party had practically covered the island and had now circled the lighthouse. Charlie started to walk toward the door when he heard Laura calling.

"Come here. Come quick!" she shouted anxiously. Her friends hurried to her side.

"Look," she pointed, her face white as milk.

"He's got rabies," said Pete.

"Oh, no!" Kerry exclaimed and moved back a couple of steps.

"Don't go near him," Andrew warned them.

Throckmorton stood still with a dull look on his face. He snorted a half-cough and shook his head. The beagle's mouth was covered with white foam. The tiger rug was still tied to his back, but rather rumpled by now.

He snorted again and began to move toward the group.

"Stay clear," said Charlie. He raised his arms to hold them back.

Throckmorton took a few quick steps in their direction and all five broke into a run. They looked like track stars running down the hill and hurdling over fallen logs. They all knelt behind a log next to their campfire and huddled together.

"Over here, over here." Charlie motioned to Kerry and Pete. "Give me one of those crab nets."

"What are you going to do?" asked Kerry.

"It's a simple plan," he explained, "but it will take all the courage you two can muster. You'll have to walk up to Throckmorton and get his attention. After that I can take over."

"Why me?" asked Kerry.

"Is that your name or something?" said Charlie in disgust—" 'Why me Kerry?' Now cool it and you won't get bit. Go ahead."

The two boys walked slowly and stiffly toward Throckmorton. Neither looked too anxious to get there.

"Here, Throckmorton," said Kerry.

"Nice boy, nice boy." Pete extended his hand slightly.

"Don't bite, boy; don't bite," Kerry pleaded.

Meanwhile Charlie raced around to get behind the beagle. His body kept disappearing as he hurried to a rock, a tree, and then a clump of grass. One end or the other of his crab net always managed to stick out.

"Just stand still, Throckmorton," said Kerry as he walked.

"Hurry, Charlie," Pete whispered. "Before he eats us both."

Throckmorton began walking slowly toward the pair. His tiger outfit looked disheveled, but no one seemed to notice.

"Gotcha!" Charlie screamed as he threw the net over Throckmorton's head and pulled back on the handle. "Jump him, guys!" he ordered.

Kerry and Pete lunged toward the beagle, but Throckmorton wouldn't stand still. He stiffened his neck and pulled Charlie for a couple of feet. Then he pivoted and threw the net off.

The second Kerry and Pete saw the net fall, they stopped dead in their tracks. Throckmorton shook his head and started chasing the two boys. Refusing to be discouraged, Charlie chased Throckmorton, his net held high as if he were hunting butterflies.

When Laura had seen all the action, she had run toward the dog, but by now had turned and retreated. Andrew decided to stay safely in a tree.

Suddenly Throckmorton stopped and turned to face Charlie. Totally surprised, Charlie stumbled to a halt.

"Hold it!" Andrew yelled. "Back off for a minute."

Charlie looked bewildered but he was happy to stop. Throckmorton stood still and coughed.

"Your dog has something caught in its throat," said Andrew as he climbed down from the tree.

Throckmorton coughed two more times and an ugly wad dropped from his mouth. Everyone came cautiously close to see what had happened.

"It was a toad," Chesapeake Charlie announced. They looked down at the green mess Throckmorton had spit on the ground. "I should have known better. This often happens if a dog eats a toad. He'll give off a white foam and look like he has rabies." Charlie patted the large beagle.

"If you knew that, why didn't you tell us?" asked Kerry.

"I forgot. Everybody forgets." Charlie began to untie the tiger rug from Throckmorton's back. "I'm sorry, old buddy. I'd rather have you for a beagle than a tiger."

The rest of the afternoon was spent playing games, talking to Andrew, and making plans for the future.

"How much longer before you think we should take you to shore, Andrew?" Laura asked.

"I hope it won't be long. However, I am afraid I should remain here until I'm reasonably sure the *Whirlwind* has left."

"Maybe Laura and Pete could check on the boat tomorrow," Charlie volunteered. "They can also keep their ears open for any news about the two men. They will be back from Deeron Island early in the morning."

"We had better start back," announced Laura, "Before my parents start looking for me."

"Pete knows how to start the motor," Charlie explained.

"Does he also know how to check the sky for thunderclouds?" she asked.

"One little mistake and you never forget," said Charlie. "Besides, those clouds came up like a 747."

"Whatever you say, but I still don't know why they call you Chesapeake. Come on, Pete."

"Have you ever been crabbing, Andrew?" asked Charlie. "This will be a great time to do it. I can teach you. Someday I'd like to get into a crab-catching contest. I bet I can beat most guys with a line and chicken wings." Charlie picked up his net. "That's how it's done. I brought some chicken along so we can catch some.

"A week ago I caught a crab with a green tag. Some scientists put tags on crabs so they can study their movements. The address was right on the tag. I talked Mom into riding down to the laboratory to return it. I could have driven the car, but I'm not old enough yet—but I know how. Anyway, they gave me three dollars for returning the tag. Not bad. I'm looking for another one now."

"You really seem to enjoy living on Chesapeake Bay," Andrew remarked.

"It's the best. I feel sorry for people who live in the middle of the country where it's flat and there's no water. I even have a secret recipe for dandelion salad. I bet you haven't had that before—have you?"

"I can't say that I have. Where did you get the recipe?" Andrew didn't sound enthusiastic.

"That's the secret. I promised not to tell."

"Here come Laura and Pete," Kerry announced.

"Big waterman, huh!" Laura began to bark before she was close to Charlie. "You think you know all about the Bay," she grumbled.

"What's wrong now?" he asked.

"The motor is out of gas," Pete explained.

"It can't be," Charlie protested. "I filled it just— well, just—a week ago."

"You are dangerous," Laura said loudly, wagging her finger at Charlie. "And what are we supposed to do now?"

"Well, I don't really know," Charlie answered humbly.

"I'll tell you what we have to do, Charlie Dean. We have to row that crate back to shore, that's what. It will be real late and poor Pete's back will probably break."

"Why *my* back?" asked the startled Pete.

"Because you wouldn't think of making a young lady row. Let's go." She motioned to Pete and headed back to the boat. Pete shrugged his shoulders and followed with a puzzled look on his face.

"Now that the children have left, we can get on with my secret recipe. This is what we'll need: dig up plenty of dandelions—get the root and all. If they look tough and old, leave them alone. We need young, tender plants."

"I'd rather eat hot dogs," Kerry complained.

"Come on, Kerry," Andrew egged him on. "Let's try a little adventure. I'd like to eat them once. We can dig together."

The three diggers talked as they worked, their conversation covering a wide range of subjects. Andrew had never seen a baseball or football game. His favorite sports were rugby, soccer, and track. He had a couple of brothers back in Solona, but his elderly parents had moved soon after the new government took over.

"You ought to settle down here," Charlie told Andrew. "You could become an aqua farmer. The Bay will yield four or five tons of vegetation an acre every year."

"That sounds tempting, but I'm not sure how much I know about underwater farming," Andrew replied.

"Now remember, Kerry," Charlie tried to sound like a college professor, "you can eat dandelion leaves, but be careful. Some leaves are poisonous. For instance, rhubarb leaves can be bad for you."

"I don't think I'll get rhubarb and dandelions confused," Kerry replied. "Rhubarb leaves are bigger, aren't they?"

"Sure thing," said Charlie. "But the point is, don't go around eating just any leaf. Same thing with the poinsettias at Christmas. You don't want to eat those either."

"Do you think we have enough by now?" Andrew asked politely. "My bucket is nearly full."

"Just one more and I'm done," Charlie replied as he dug deeply to reach as much of the root as he could. "That's a nice thick one," he exclaimed as he held it up like a prized trophy.

They carried their harvest to the campfire and began to prepare the greens on the large fallen log.

"Cut the roots off but don't throw them away.

Then we need to wash both leaves and roots until they're spotless," Charlie ordered.

Soon the leaves and sliced roots were boiling in a pot on the open fire. Charlie removed it from the fire and gave each person a large paper plate full.

"Put some of this on it if you want." Charlie passed a package of bacon bits and a bottle of salad dressing.

"It does taste good," Andrew said, gleaming.

"Sure it does," Charlie agreed.

"Well," Kerry picked at his food, "I've tasted worse."

"We have nearly two hours before dark." Andrew looked at the sky. "I'd like to look for that treasure a little longer."

"Hey, me too," said Charlie. "I'm almost finished." He took another large forkful of greens.

"Do you really think there is treasure on this island?" asked Kerry.

"Of course, I don't know," answered Andrew, "but I have to admit the map looks real. I understand the bottle Charlie found is certainly old."

"I don't have any doubt about it," Charlie mumbled with his mouth full.

"Charlie says the Chesapeake Bay was big pirate territory," Kerry added.

"It was such a feared place," Charlie switched to his deep voice, "that ships would wait near Barbados until there were half a dozen or more. They were too scared to sail the Bay alone."

"What ended the pirate menace?" asked Andrew.

"Too many pirates were hanged," Charlie explained. "The last big one was William Fly in 1726.

They handed him a bunch of flowers called a nosegay, preached a sermon, and then hanged him high."

"It sounds exciting," said Andrew. "Let's get back to digging. I thought we should try by this huge dead tree. For one thing, it's probably the oldest tree on the island and for another, it looks like the X on the map was just slightly more in this direction."

After a quick cleanup, the trio gathered their tools and climbed into the hole. Not only was the crevice deep, but it had been dug widely and all three men could easily fit. Shovels flew in several directions like swimmers' arms arching out of the water. The diggers said little during the next hour. The noise from their tools and the exhausting labor made it hard to be heard.

"Let's quit," Kerry finally insisted. He dropped his shovel and leaned back against the side of the hole.

"It's too soon," said Charlie. His voice had a happy ring to it.

"It may be too late for my back," Kerry groaned.

"Just take a look at this!" Charlie sounded excited. Andrew and Kerry pushed in close to where Charlie stood.

"It's a stone," said Kerry.

"Maybe not." Andrew looked closer. "It could be a piece of pottery."

All three diggers dropped to their knees and began to dig around the object. Kerry used a stick and Andrew a piece of rock. Charlie pulled at the ground with his shovel handle.

"It's thick," Kerry observed as they began to make progress.

"It might be made from bone," Andrew speculated.

"Look! Look!" said Charlie excitedly.

"What is it?" asked Kerry.

They had uncovered a hole at one end of the object. It looked like an eye socket.

"It's a skull," Andrew announced.

"Ugh," said Kerry.

Both boys drew their hands back from the gruesome bone. For a minute no one said a word. Without realizing it, Charlie looked around to see if anyone was watching them.

"He looks like he's winking at us," said Charlie.

"Let's dig the rest of him out." Andrew took his stick and continued scraping dirt away. As the boys helped him the second eye socket appeared, and then the hole where the nose had been. Finally they uncovered the large teeth which filled the open mouth. Charlie picked up the skull and held it out at arms' length.

"He must have been an ugly pirate," Charlie said.

"Well, how do you suppose he got here?" wondered Kerry.

"Don't you know?" Charlie replied. "Lots of times the pirates would force people to dig these holes and then kill them so they couldn't tell anyone."

"That's possible," Andrew agreed. "But then, it could just be a grave."

"That gives me the creeps," said Kerry. "Now we're grave robbers."

"Nonsense," said Charlie. "We've found it. This is pirate's loot." He pushed his shovel back into the ground and pounded his foot firmly against it. "Bet we'll find the treasure before the sun is completely gone."

The sound of shovels slicing through dirt was the

only noise that came out of the hole during the next half hour. As the sun sank into the Bay arms flew faster and dirt sailed swiftly through the air.

"Hey, I've hit something over here," Andrew announced. He scraped some more dirt off his new find.

"What is it?" asked Charlie.

"I don't know yet, but it's dark."

Chapter Seven

Early the next morning Laura hurried over to the Dean house on her bike.

"I think I've got a way to help Andrew," Laura suggested to Pete. "We need to keep those two guys busy for at least another day. Their ship can't stay here much longer."

"What've you got up your sleeve?" Pete asked.

"I don't have the plan entirely worked out yet, but I've been thinking. The ferryboat returns from Deeron Island at 8:45—I called to make sure. That gives us half an hour to get to the dock and prepare for action."

"But I have to be careful," said Pete. "Those guys will recognize me from the skating rink."

"That's no problem. Grab your hat and a pair of sunglasses. We're going to have to move fast."

While Pete ran upstairs to fetch his things, Laura went into the kitchen.

"Mrs. Dean, do you have a couple of straws I could use?" she asked.

"Certainly," she replied. "They should be in that first drawer to your left."

Laura and Pete mounted their bikes and were at the dock in a few quick minutes. They could see the short, white ferryboat approaching only a hundred yards away.

"Our only hope is to keep them confused and running," Laura explained. "If they catch on to what we're doing, Andrew could be in big trouble. I'll stay on one side and you stay in the tank." She pointed to a green trash can.

The two men leaped from the boat. Both looked angry and determined as they hustled down the dock.

Whack! The tall man grabbed the back of his neck. Whack! His hand raced for the other side of his face.

"What was that?" he asked his short partner as they halted in the middle of the street.

"Ouch!" The man's head jerked backwards. "It must be bees."

The two continued their brisk walk but only moved two steps before they were hit again. This time the short man swung around. He found himself staring squarely at a young lady in blue jeans, holding a straw. Laura stuck her tongue out at the man.

"Why, you punk!" said the short man, and started to chase her.

"Hold it!" shouted his partner. "We aren't here to chase children."

While they stood arguing, Laura raised her straw and sent a bean flying against the tall man's chest.

"You runt!" the tall one grunted, and both men began to chase her. Laura took off, looking back once to make sure they were coming.

Whack! Whack! each man was hit again as they ran down the street. They stopped abruptly.

"Where is that coming from?" asked the short man. They looked around but saw no children. The tall one stared for a moment at the green trash can across the street, but thought nothing of it.

Whack! Laura had reappeared at the corner.

"What's wrong? Your feet glued to the ground?" she taunted. "Try it this way." Laura jumped in the air and wiggled her feet in a pretend run.

Whack! Another bean hit the short one from the side. He took another quick glance at the trash can.

"Forget the can; let's catch that girl." They began to run full speed toward the corner. As they turned, they spotted Laura approaching the entrance of a large department store.

They stopped again.

"We can't go in there," the tall one insisted.

"You're right." The short one straightened out his clothes and pulled his jacket into place. "We have to get back to our search." They turned their backs and walked away.

"Wait a minute." The tall one bent over to tie his shoe. "Ouch!" he shouted as he jumped up like a jack-in-the-box. His eyes were large from pain and his hands rubbed his seat.

They both turned to see Laura standing barely twenty feet away. Straining with all their might, they lunged toward her as she sped off toward the department store.

Bounding between cars, the two men darted across the street and sprinted through the large doors. They halted clumsily inside the spacious furniture department. Long, plush sofas, overstuffed chairs, luxurious drapes and rolls of colorful carpets filled the room.

"We've lost her," muttered the tall man as they peered around the room.

Whack! The short one grabbed his leg.

"Over there," he pointed, "behind that green sofa."

They had taken only two steps toward the sofa when the tall man felt a sharp pain on the back of his neck.

"Ouch!" he shouted. "There's someone behind us."

A store salesman looked up at the odd pair, and frowned at them.

"Forget that," the short man insisted. "Let's get that girl."

When they arrived at the first row of sofas, they checked to the left and right but saw no one.

"You go down that aisle and I'll head down this one. Keep low."

The short man dropped to his knees and started to crawl down the row. A few feet away his partner walked cautiously, searching for his attacker. The short man's knees and hands pounded against the carpet as he scurried along. Suddenly, he stopped. Below his downcast eyes were two large black shoes. His eyes traveled up along a pair of gray trousers. As his eyes pointed up, he saw an angry man with his hands on his hips. It was the salesman.

"Are you looking for some furniture?" he asked sharply. The short man pulled himself up and tried to smile.

"I lost a button off my coat," he said sheepishly.

"Your jacket has a zipper," the salesman replied dryly.

"Oh, oh, of course. How silly of me." The short man pushed past the salesman and shuffled into the next room with his friend close behind.

"Now, let's forget these pesky kids," advised the tall man, "and get out of here before we get into real trouble."

Without another word they started looking for an exit.

"It's over this way," the tall man motioned.

Whack! A bean hit him in the neck.

"That's it!" His face turned red with anger. "I'm going to tear that runt in half."

The two hurried toward the children's clothing section to find the bean sniper.

"It came from in here," said the tall man. He began to pull the hangers apart among the girls' dresses.

"Were you looking for anything in particular?" asked the gentle voice of the saleslady.

"We're looking for a brat with a bean shooter," the short man replied gruffly.

"I'll have to ask you to not mess up the dresses," she warned.

Whack! A bean smacked against the back of the short man's pants. He whirled quickly but saw no one. They ran up the aisle for a few feet but soon realized there was no one in sight. They stopped beside three boy manikins and panted like thirsty puppies. One of the manikins was wearing a hat and sunglasses. Neither noticed that it was holding a straw. Pete knew he didn't dare twitch.

"Hey!" a girl's voice grabbed their attention. "Over here, fat feet!"

They darted toward Laura. As they ran at full speed, Laura pushed a short clothing cart in front of them. The tall man flipped over the cart and tumbled onto the floor. His short partner fell into a basket and sent it spinning in circles.

When the cart came to a halt, two men in blue uniforms were standing beside them.

"What kind of a game are you two playing?" one policeman asked gruffly.

"It isn't us, officers," the tall man protested. "It's those kids."

"I don't see any kids," said the policeman. "Maybe you two had better come into the office and answer some questions."

"When they come out," Laura told Pete, "we can still follow them, but we have to be careful. If they get their hands on us, we could be in big trouble."

"All right, but don't forget, we have to get back to the island."

"Our bikes will give us a fast getaway." Laura patted the handlebars.

"Man, the police must be really giving those guys a going over," said Pete. "The bank clock says 10:30."

Fifteen minutes later the two men came out of the store. The police escorted them to the sidewalk where they parted company. None of them smiled.

The men walked briskly across the street.

"They're going to take off!" Pete exclaimed to Laura.

"No, they're not; look, they've stopped."

"What are those nuts arguing about?" wondered Pete out loud.

"Good thing. At least they're confused," said Laura.

"They've pulled some papers out of their pockets," Pete noted.

"Let's sit still until we see what they're up to," Laura suggested.

"They're stopping people on the street," observed Pete.

"They must be desperate," Laura concluded. "If they're still asking people on the street, they have no idea where Andrew is. Time's on our side. They have to get back to the ship sometime."

"Time, time," Pete muttered. "Do you want to buy some more time?"

"I don't know, Pete. Maybe we've bugged those guys long enough."

"We can't settle for half a job. I have an idea that might send them back to the ship a little earlier."

"Let's hear it," Laura gave in. "But don't make it something dumb."

"It's the perfect plan. First, let's duck into the toy store. Better put the lock back on your bike!"

Ten minutes later the two men were still making their way slowly down the street. They stopped as many people as they could and showed them Andrew's picture. No one gave them much encouragement. A few people were impatient and merely brushed on past them. The men were gruff and most people didn't care to talk to them for long. Even when the men smiled and tried to be polite, their rough manners were obvious.

"Don't jiggle that box so much," warned Pete.

"I know how to carry a box." Laura forced a pretend grin.

"Well, don't get huffy. I just don't want to mess up this perfect plan. Let's put the boxes here near the ledge."

Laura and Pete knelt down and carefully poked their heads above the edge of the roof.

"There they are," whispered Laura.

"But they're moving past us," Pete explained. "We'll have to move down and wait for them to come to us."

Cautiously they dragged their boxes to the roof of the next building. The duo settled in and looked for their prey.

"Here they come," said Pete gleefully, "and at just the right pace."

"They're sitting ducks," Laura giggled. "They take a few steps, and then stop and talk. Wait until Charlie hears about this. He'll eat his heart out."

"Remember, not until I say Geronimo," Pete instructed her. "Here they come."

Pete picked up a bulging, quivering water-filled balloon. Its green sides were stretched nearly to the bursting point. Laura's red water bomb looked like a flabby beach ball.

"Don't fire until you see the points on their heads," Pete whispered. "Not yet."

"Just a few more feet," said Laura.

The two men stopped to talk to a lady. As they showed her Andrew's picture, a voice above them excitedly whispered, "Geronimo!" A plump green balloon sailed through the air. It splattered against the chest of the tall man, soaking his jacket and drenching the photograph in his hand.

His surprised partner looked up to see what had

happened. Just as he focused his eyes toward the sky, a wobbling red balloon crashed into his upturned face.

Both men began to shout angrily in their own language. Laura and Pete didn't try to figure out the conversation, but merely heaved two more balloons over the ledge. One hit the tall man across the back and the second blasted the bewildered lady standing next to them.

"Aaah!" she screamed. "Is this some kind of a joke?" She walloped the short man with her shopping bag.

While the short man tried to dodge the lady's powerful swings, the tall man looked up to try and get a glimpse of his attackers. He shook his fist at the enemy he couldn't see. As he stood making menacing motions, a stranger approached him.

"Are you guys on Candid Camera?" the man asked. Before anyone could reply, four balloons sailed down from the roof. A round red balloon hit the stranger's arm. The lady screamed as a green bomb exploded on her graying head. The two men managed to dodge the other balloons, but the short one walked into a balloon as it burst on the ground. The splash soaked his trousers.

"Run!" the stranger shouted. Six more water bombs came hurling through the sky. All of the weapons missed as everyone quickly backed away from the building.

"Who is it?" asked a spectator.

"A couple of brats," the soaked lady fumed.

Without a word the two men dashed between two buildings and headed for the alley.

"Over here," called the tall man as he pointed toward the fire escape. "Help me with this ladder."

The two men grabbed the metal ladder and pulled it down.

"We better get out of here," Pete warned Laura.

"Not so soon," she objected. "We still have that second box of balloons."

"Hurry! They're coming fast," warned Pete.

"Just don't panic," assured Laura. "We can still get away."

They carried their boxes to the back of the building and crouched above the fire escape.

"Let them get a little closer," Laura suggested.

"There they are!" shouted the short man scurrying up the stairs.

"Geronimo!" Laura yelled.

Balloons flew over the side like a colorful snowstorm. Smash, smack, crash, splatter. Nearly a dozen balloons rained down on the horrified victims. They managed to sidestep a few bombs, but nearly half found their targets. To finish it off, Pete hurled their empty boxes down the stairs.

"Let's go!" Laura commanded.

They darted across the roof and bounded over a small brick wall. Racing over two more buildings, they came to a second fire escape and clambered down. Just before they reached the ground the two men appeared on the roof above them. Without hesitating, Laura and Pete ran down the alley and out of sight.

"That was too close," said Pete as they pedaled their bikes toward home.

"Wait until we tell Charlie what we did!" Laura exclaimed between breaths. "He won't even believe us."

As they passed Beachwood Drive, they both leaned back and rode without holding the handle bars. With broad smiles on their faces, they made the trip home in record time.

"I hate to leave those two dodos," said Pete. "We could have played a lot more tricks on them."

"That was plenty," Laura sat up proudly on her speeding bike. "This way we can still get to the island by noon."

They wheeled into Pete's driveway and bounced roughly over the grass into the backyard. Not bothering to use their kickstands, they dropped their vehicles and ran toward the back porch.

"Mom!" Pete yelled as they scrambled into the kitchen.

"Slow down," Mrs. Dean said with her hands held in front of her. "You two are acting like a couple of cyclones. What have you been up to?"

"Not a thing," said Laura.

"Just a little shooting practice." Pete was about to break into laughter.

"Maybe a little bomb practice, too," Laura added with a very suspicious smile.

"Can we pack some lunch?" asked Pete. "We need to get back to Randolph Island."

Laura and Pete pitched in to help Mrs. Dean collect and prepare the food. Pete slapped peanut butter and grape jelly on fresh white bread. Laura mixed some cherry drink and closed the plastic jug tightly. Mrs. Dean fried half a dozen oyster fritters that she already had mixed up. The strong smell filled the kitchen and made everyone's taste buds stand up on end.

Their saliva began to flow freely.

"Man, that smells good," said Pete.

"Well, here," Mrs. Dean offered warmly. "Why don't you two split one? It's a long trip across to the island."

Mrs. Dean put the oyster fritter on a small plate and cut it in half with a fork. The freshly fried fritter sent up a puff of steam and its strong, rich aroma. As hot as it was, neither Laura nor Pete lost any time snapping it up. They chewed it thoroughly, savoring each piece of tangy flavor.

"One more?" Pete begged.

"All right." Mrs. Dean was happy to cooperate. "I can fry a few more."

Pete grabbed a couple of handfuls of chocolate chip cookies from the chubby bear jar.

"That's enough," said Mrs. Dean. "You already have enough food to feed Mongolia."

"Just Upper Mongolia," Pete kidded, "but I guess it will have to do."

"Hurry back!" Mrs. Dean handed Laura and Pete each a large bag of food. "And tell Charlie we expect all of you home tonight."

Pete and Laura made sure the motor had plenty of gas. They even took an extra gallon can, just in case they ran out. The engine revved up smoothly and the happy pair started out across the Bay.

"That's them for sure," said the tall man sitting in the car. He held a pair of black binoculars. The collar curled up on his wet shirt.

"Keep the glasses on them," the short man ordered his partner as he made notes on his small pad.

"They are heading north-by-northeast. I'll check the map and see what's out there."

"Their boat is heading straight as an arrow." The tall man didn't budge his binoculars.

"That's enough," the short man ordered. "Let's go and rent a boat."

"Don't get too close to the crabber," Laura warned Pete.

"I'm nowhere near him."

Pete had plenty of his brother's love for the Bay. He had spent a couple of days on a crabbing boat, and that rich, brackish crab smell was still fresh in his memory. Actually he had spent more nights than days, since crabbers begin their work at three a.m.

"He's pulling up pots," Pete called to Laura.

The pots looked lightweight, but he could remember how heavy they were. A pot looks like a wire cage, but filled with crabs it weighs thirty to forty pounds.

Crabs swim into the bottom of the pot looking for food and don't know how to get out. They naturally swim up to get away and find no exits there. Twice a day, the crabber pulls up each pot and empties it. The busy waterman places nearly a hundred crab pots in the water.

Pete had trouble keeping up when he worked on the boat. Pulling up pots and emptying them was all he could handle.

"See those black gloves he's wearing? If he didn't have those, the crabs would tear his fingers up. They're quick and can see all around themselves."

Bushel baskets and wire mesh pots were stacked high on the short white boat. Radio antennae stuck up from the captain's roof and a small rowboat lay across the bow.

"When I grow up I just might become a crabber," said Pete. "It isn't much money, but it's great work!"

Chapter Eight

Kerry sat disgustedly above the hole. "So far our treasure consists of one skull, three bones, and part of an old black boot," he muttered. "My back's killing me."

"How can you sit there?" Charlie asked. "If we found these things there must be real treasure nearby." Charlie tossed another spadeful.

"You bet, Charlie," Kerry smirked. "Where there is junk you are likely to find more junk. I think that was Einstein's theory of junk."

"Kerry could be right," Andrew added. "Part of the island has washed away during the past 200 years. Plus, I suppose pirates often robbed each other. But I have to admit it is fun to dig and hope."

"Fun to dig?" Kerry ridiculed. "Only if you're a ground hog."

Clunk.

"I hit something!" Charlie yelled. "I hit something!" His voice rose higher as Andrew came close to look.

"It might be the top of a crate," said Andrew.

"It's probably an old box of prune juice," snapped Kerry.

Charlie and Andrew excitedly carved away at the earth around the mysterious object. The dirt was packed solid and refused to move easily.

"Whatever it is, it's huge," said Chesapeake Charlie without slowing a stroke of his shovel. "This crate must be three feet deep," he exaggerated.

Curiosity had gotten the best of Kerry and he jumped into the hole. His shovel joined the others' in uncovering the wooden mystery.

Old English letters began to appear as they dug. The first letter was a large, fancy "O," the second looked like an "L."

"Don't chip the wood," warned Charlie. "It'll be worth more if the box is in one piece."

The ground started to surrender its treasure. The crate was a faded brown and the branded lettering read, "Oliver's Wine and Spirits."

"It's a crate of old booze," Kerry concluded. "If it isn't empty."

"Maybe they just used this box," Charlie hoped, "and they stuffed it with pearls and gold."

"And maybe I'm the King of Spain," Kerry chirped.

"Just dig," said Charlie.

Finally they freed the old box and pulled it from the ancient grave. They set the crate upright and inside they could see six large olive green bottles. The crate lid was missing and each bottle was packed down with dirt. Charlie and Andrew took sticks and began to dig around the bottles.

"There's nothing in them," said Kerry. "They're filled with dirt."

"That does seem true," Andrew added.

"Well, I s'pose we can at least get the deposit back on them," Kerry joked.

"Don't laugh," Charlie protested. "These bottles could be worth big money. Besides, we've only started to dig."

"Not me," said Kerry. "I'm through. What are you going to dig for—bottle caps?" He rolled back laughing as hard as he could. "Don't you get it? Bottle caps."

"I get it," snarled Charlie. "The moths are eating your brain."

"Got it," said Andrew cheerfully. He lifted a bottle to eye level. It had a long neck and then stretched out into a wide bell-bottom. "That dirt makes them heavy," he added.

They soon had all six bottles free and brushed the dirt off the outside.

"Look at the bottom of this one," Charlie said excitedly. "It says 1718. It's beautiful. Let's wash them out."

Each person took two bottles and they carried them to the beach. Carefully they began to clean them out by digging into the bottles with sticks and rinsing each one several times.

"Guess who's coming," said Kerry. In the distance they could faintly see a motorboat heading toward the island. It was still too far away to hear.

The next half-hour was spent laughing about their adventures and kidding. Charlie, Kerry, and Andrew told stories of their exciting treasure hunt. Laura and Pete alternated between snickers and fits of laughter as they told about their water and bean wars.

"So, where do you think the men are now?" asked Charlie.

"They're probably back at the ship getting dry clothes," answered Laura. "And boy were they mad."

"I think the Eastern Shore has seen the last of them," Pete added.

"We have to make plans to take Andrew to the police," Charlie began. "When do you think would be a good time, Andrew?"

"Maybe tomorrow," Andrew answered. "That's probably as long as the *Whirlwind* dares to stay in the Bay. I think it's almost time to venture out."

"But what will happen to you?" Kerry asked.

"If your government agrees to let me stay, I have an uncle in Ohio whom I can stay with. I'll be all right."

"Promise you'll give us your address," said Laura.

"We'd like to come visit you," Pete added.

"Yeah, and to have you come visit us, too," Charlie insisted.

"I won't forget what the four of you have done to help me. I might have starved if it hadn't been for your kindness. God must have sent that treasure map to you so that you would find me."

"You've made me realize how prejudiced I've been," Kerry confessed. "Sometimes people can get some crazy ideas in their heads. Wait till I tell my uncle about you."

"It makes a big difference if you get to know people," said Andrew. "Not just to see them, but to sit down and listen to them. Many times we dislike people we don't even know."

"You'd think Christians would be better at understanding others," Laura remarked.

"Often they are," said Andrew. "But not always. I

think that's why Christ talked a good deal about Samaritans. They were of a different nationality but Jesus loved them. Also, the Roman soldiers were hated by many, but He healed a centurion's servant."

"I've thought of a great way to split our treasure," Charlie announced.

"First, I want my five dollars back," Kerry interrupted.

"Don't worry, you'll get it," Charlie assured. "But here's what we'll do: Everyone gets one bottle, except Andrew; he gets two. It will probably be big money."

Everyone nodded enthusiastically.

"What about the rest of the treasure?" asked Pete.

"You mean the skull and the boot?" Charlie joked.

"What skull?" asked Pete, his eyes big as golf balls.

"Come on over here," directed Charlie. "I'll show you the skull and crossbones we found."

"Don't lie to me," said Laura. "People don't find real skulls and crossbones."

"Ha, ha, ha!" Kerry used his most horrible laugh. "Just you wait and see, little lady." He rubbed his hands fiendishly.

"Let's race to the hole. But first give the bottles to Andrew," commanded Charlie. "Will you hold them for us?"

"I'd be glad to."

"Line up behind this mark." Charlie made a line on the ground with the heel of his shoe. He then joined the trio.

"I'll say when to go," said Kerry.

"Get out of here. You'll cheat," Pete protested.

"Why don't we ask Andrew to count to three for

us?" asked Laura.

"Fine," said Andrew. "One—"

"Back up," Kerry told Pete.

"Two—"

"Are you allowed to hunch over?" asked Laura.

"Thr—"

"What's that?" asked Charlie.

"Rats!" shouted Kerry as he jerked forward. "I was ready to go."

"Shhh! Listen," Charlie said urgently.

They all turned toward the water and saw a white dot moving in their direction.

"It's a boat," said Charlie.

"There are lots of boats on the Bay," Kerry shrugged. "Let's race."

"You don't suppose?" asked Laura.

"I don't know," said Charlie, "but it's heading directly for us. We can't take any chances. Whoever it is will be here in just a few minutes."

"If it's them, they're looking for Pete and me," said Laura. "They don't know Andrew is here."

"That's it," Charlie snapped. "Can you two make our boat move fast?"

"Of course," said Pete.

"I mean enough to outrun that boat coming?" Charlie asked excitedly.

"We better go quickly," said Laura as she started toward the boat.

"Give them the runaround," Charlie ordered. "If they follow you, we can hide Andrew and they won't even stop here."

Laura and Pete broke into a run for the beach. Kerry, Andrew, and Charlie didn't wait to hear the boat start. They ran to the lighthouse. Just as they entered the door, they heard the motor sputter.

"It won't start!" yelled Pete.

"Pull, Pete, pull!" shouted Andrew.

"They're gaining," said Charlie.

Sputter, sputter.

"They're going to get caught!" Kerry put his hands over his eyes.

Roar! The motor revved up and Laura and Pete took off with their pursuers just a few hundred yards away. Fortunately, Laura and Pete had the faster vessel and shot away from the shore.

"Go, go!" yelled Andrew.

"Take off!" Kerry waved his fist.

"Stay low," warned Charlie. "We don't want them to see us."

"They're slowing down," said the surprised Andrew.

"They aren't chasing Laura and Pete," said Charlie.

"Nuts, they *are* stopping here," exclaimed Kerry.

"We've had it, unless we can think of something in a hurry," said Charlie. "They've cut their motor and are paddling in. Close that door tightly."

The two men came in close to the shore and climbed out. They pulled their boat safely onto the beach and looked around.

"There's a path," said the tall man. Each pulled a foot-long black rubber club from inside his belt. Snapping them loudly against their palms, they hurried onto the beach.

"I've got it," whispered Kerry. "Let's stand behind the door; when they come in we can jump them."

"Maybe," said Charlie. "But they look tough. What if they beat our heads in?"

"There is really only one thing to do, friends." Andrew sounded hopeless. "I'm the one they are looking for. If I give myself up they won't bother you." He reached for the doorknob.

"Never!" Kerry pulled Andrew's hand back.

"Kerry's right," Charlie whispered. "We aren't licked and we aren't about to be."

"I hope your hunch is right," said the short man as they walked cautiously across the sand. Every few steps he slapped his palm with the rubber club.

"It's just a feeling, but why else would those kids try to bug us?" asked the tall one.

"Yeah, but what if they are hiding him on some other island? He certainly wasn't in the boat when they took off."

"And you know why?" Smack, smack. The tall man hit his hand with his club. "Because they left him here alone. They were just decoys to make us chase them."

"How are we going to flush him out?" asked the short man.

"It's easy. We can see the entire island from here. First, we make sure he isn't on the beaches. If he isn't, he has to be in the old lighthouse."

"Sounds good. How do we check the beaches?"

"Nothing to it," the tall man reasoned. "I can see both the lighthouse and the beach from here. I'll stand here while you run around the beach. If he's here, you will flush him out and I'll be right here to help you."

"I have to run all around the island?" the short man's eyes bulged.

"You know you're a better runner than I am."

"But—but what if he's hiding and jumps me?"

"No problem," the tall man explained. "If he jumps you, just yell and I'm at your side like a bullet. Hurry, man, run."

The short man took off in a swift jog. His face was a cross between confusion and anger. Looking like an eagle, the tall man glanced from side to side ready to pounce on anything that moved.

Fortunately for the short man Randolph Island wasn't too large. In a few minutes he came back, pumping his legs and panting like a thirsty dog.

"Did you see anything?" asked the tall man.

"I—I—I—"

"Speak up. Did you see a ghost?"

"I—"

"What was it, man?"

"I—I can't breathe."

"You ought to get into shape," said the tall man. "If trouble starts I'm ready, and you're panting like a wounded moose. Follow me."

The pair started toward the lighthouse.

"He must be inside. We'd better stick together. If we have to fight him, you won't have a chance alone."

Half skipping, the tired short man struggled to keep up. As they reached the front door, the men slouched down and stepped cautiously.

"Don't make a sound," the tall man ordered. "You had better go in first."

"Why me?" the short man whined.

"Suppose he jumps you," he explained. "Then I can barge right in and knock him down. If he jumps me, you're too tired to rescue me."

"Oh," the short man grunted. He pushed carefully

against the door, causing its shakey hinges to squeak as it opened. The room was almost totally dark except for the small amount of light the open door allowed. The tall man followed his partner inside with his club held high.

"I don't see anything," whispered the short man.

"That looks like another room. You lead the way."

"Why don't you lead?"

"You know why."

"I know, I'm out of shape."

"What was that?" whispered the tall man.

"I don't know, but it sounds like someone is upstairs."

"Don't worry. I'm right behind you."

The short man inched forward.

They began to climb the old wooden steps. Each step creaked and sagged under the men's weight.

"There's some light from that window," whispered the tall man. "Keep your club high."

"I don't see anything," said the short man.

"Go on," his partner urged.

"I heard something," the short man hesitated. "There it is again."

"We aren't afraid, are we?" Both men were shaking like Jello on a lawn mower.

"Wha—what's that?" asked the short man.

"It—looks like a tiger!"

"Growl, growl." The menacing noise roared down the stairs.

"Aaah! Aaah!" The men stumbled into each other as they bolted down the stairs. As fast as they could scramble, both darted through one room and into another.

"Growl, growl," the terrible sound echoed after them. They crashed into the door and staggered outside.

Two frightened men raced across the island. When they reached the beach, both dove off the small cliff onto the sand. When they sat up they were still shaking.

"I don't think our guy was in that lighthouse," said the tall man. "What do you think?"

"I—I—I," said the short man trying to catch his breath. "I don't think so either."

"Let's go find those kids."

"Great idea," said the short man.

Without another word they lunged toward the boat. After two nervous pulls on the cord, the motor started and the vessel jerked forward at high speed.

Kerry, Andrew, and Charlie stood in the dark laughing so hard that tears ran down their faces. Each took turns patting Throckmorton, as he wagged his tail beneath the silly rug.

"He's a great tiger-beagle," said Charlie.

"Those guys are probably swimming across the Bay by now," chuckled Kerry.

"Wait till I tell Laura," said Charlie. "She made fun of my tiger-beagle. Growl, growl."

When the sound of the engine seemed far enough away, they all stepped out of the lighthouse. They were still laughing and kidding Throckmorton.

"What are you guys doing?" shouted Pete as he and Laura walked up from the other side of the island.

"Where did you two come from?" asked Kerry.

"When we saw they weren't following us, we just circled around and came up the other way," Laura explained. "We knew you would need us."

"Well, we didn't," Charlie bragged. "Tiger-beagle rescued us all by himself." He brushed his hands across Throckmorton's floppy ears.

"Cruelty to animals," Laura protested. "The poor dog won't know what kind of beast he is."

"Don't call Throckmorton a beast," Charlie complained. "He's a sensitive individual."

"Take that rag rug off him," Laura ordered.

"No matter what you think," Kerry interjected. "The important thing is that those two tough guys thought he was a real tiger."

Everyone looked out at the Bay, watching the boat disappear in the distance.

"We won't see those clowns again," Charlie boasted.

"I wish we could be sure," said Andrew.

"You don't really think they would come back after that, do you?" said the surprised Charlie.

"I know they don't give up easily." Andrew stared out into the Bay. "I won't really feel safe until I know they're gone for good."

"Tonight could be very important," said Charlie. "Kerry and I will have to stay here again. Pete, you and Laura go back and explain it to our parents. But don't tell them too much."

"Why do girls and little kids always have to go home?" Laura whined.

"Who's a little kid?" Pete barked.

"You are, you little whimp," answered Laura.

"I can throw you in the Bay," Pete threatened.

"Quit that," Charlie commanded. "You two can fight later. This time, don't clown around. Be here first thing in the morning."

"We don't clown around," said Laura. "We were engaged in a real war!"

"Take off," said Charlie, "before I start another war."

Chapter Nine

Early the next morning Pete and Laura returned to Randolph Island.

"Boy, are the folks mad at you," said Pete. "Dad almost drove the boat over to get you last night."

"That's all right," Charlie replied. "When we can explain the situation to them, they'll understand. Did you hear anything about our two visitors?"

"Not a word," Laura answered. "But that doesn't say much. They had already been through our neighborhood earlier. I won't be surprised if they come back out today to check these islands, though."

"But not this one," Kerry joined in. "They'd be too afraid of tiger-beagle."

"I don't want to spoil your victory party," Andrew cautioned; "but there is another possibility. The next time they may come back with guns. Then they won't be afraid of tiger-beagle or anything else."

"They wouldn't dare," Charlie insisted "Even those clowns wouldn't go around shooting people in the United States. They'd be in more trouble than they could handle."

"I hope you're correct. But I would still feel better if you would all get off the island for a couple of days," Andrew pleaded.

"Not a chance, Andrew, old buddy," said Kerry.

"We're with you all the way."

"They won't be back," Charlie said bravely, "but let's not take any chances. We need to put a good lookout in the crow's nest."

"What's a crow's nest?" asked Pete.

"You know," said Charlie. "That's pirate talk. We need to put someone up in that tree to look out for boats. The minute he sees any vessel heading this way he'll shout down."

"What dummy is going to sit up in a tree?" Pete wondered.

Charlie looked his brother in the eyes and grinned.

"Do you see anything yet, Pete?" Kerry yelled up.

"There are a lot of little white boats, but none are heading this way," Pete hollered back. "There's also one large ship, but it's far away."

While Pete peered around the Bay, his friends went back to digging for treasure. After two hours of labor all their work yielded was backaches and sore muscles. The hole was becoming wide as well as deep, and all four people could fit comfortably.

"Digging is boring," said Kerry.

"If you'd work as hard as you complain, we'd probably find all the lost gold of the English crown," Laura taunted.

"I've worked a lot harder than you," Kerry barked back. "All you do is take cruises back and forth across the Bay."

"We risked our necks slowing those two guys down," said Laura.

"Hold it!" shouted Andrew. A huge smile covered his face. "What is this?"

They all stared down at a black object just barely exposed in the dirt. For a few seconds no one moved. Then suddenly Charlie began to dig around their newest discovery.

"Don't tell me it's another boot," said Kerry.

"Not this time," said Charlie. "This baby is made of metal."

"It's a leg iron," Laura announced when Charlie picked it up. The hinge was rusted motionless and the lock would not close. Nearly a foot of heavy chain was attached.

"They probably kept a few prisoners," said Charlie. "They didn't usually take people alive, but I guess they saved a few."

"You don't suppose that lock belonged to this fellow, do you?" Charlie pointed to the skull sitting beside the hole.

"Very probably," said Andrew.

"Ugh," said Kerry. "What a way to go."

"Ship ahoy!" shouted Pete. "Heading due south," he added dramatically.

"What kind?" asked Laura.

"A big one," Pete replied.

Charlie looked over the edge of the hole. "Man, it *is* a big one!"

"Pete, come down. Do it now!" commanded Andrew.

"Is it your ship?" asked Charlie.

"Yes, it's the *Whirlwind*," said Andrew.

"Everyone duck down," said Charlie.

"Nothing to worry about," Kerry reassured. "They're heading out to sea."

"It's hard to tell. They could be making one last

stop here before they go," Andrew speculated. "Watch carefully to see if they lower a boat."

Complete silence covered the group. The gigantic ship kept plowing silently toward Randolph Island.

"It *is* getting closer," said Charlie solemnly.

"Don't panic," insisted Laura.

"No doubt about it. It's my ship."

"This is our plan. If we see anything come off that ship, we all take off for the outboard," explained Charlie. "This time you have to come with us, Andrew. If they come now, they're liable to send half a dozen men and they'll mean business."

"They're almost even with the island," observed Laura.

"Go on by," whispered Kerry. "Go on by."

Andrew closed his eyes and pleaded softly, "Lord, you've brought me this far. Please don't let us down now." Kerry looked at him uneasily, then closed his eyes too.

"They are even with us," said Laura. "Dead even."

"There's a bunch of people at the stern doing something," Pete observed. "I wonder if they're going to lower a boat."

Everyone held his breath. No one moved or spoke.

Laura finally spoke. "We better run for it."

"No, no," said Charlie excitedly. "The boat isn't being lowered. They're going on by. They're going on by!" his voice rose sharply.

"They are! They really are!" shouted Laura. She grabbed Charlie and hugged him. Charlie pushed away clumsily, his face red with embarrassment.

Kerry and Andrew opened their eyes to see the

ship moving past. Both smiled widely and then embraced in a gigantic hug. Pete was so happy he ruffled Throckmorton's ears.

"We're going home, Andrew. I want my parents to meet you," Charlie called out.

It didn't take them long to collect their tools, food, treasure, and other equipment. Kerry volunteered to tie the life preserver on Throckmorton. Laura and Andrew walked around the island one last time to make sure they didn't leave anything. They took their time to make sure not even a scrap of paper littered the island.

While everyone else was busy, Charlie wrote a note on a piece of cardboard and anchored it by the hole with two large rocks. The note read:

> Do not tarry.
> Be quick as a flea
> For you tempt the spirit,
> Of Chesapeake Charlie.

Charlie looked at the note one more time. A smug grin of satisfaction crept over his face.

The heavily loaded motorboat struggled across the Bay, heading for Charlie's house. Hardly anyone spoke during the trip. They were all extremely happy and terribly tired.

"You won't believe half of our story, Woody." Charlie and Laura had brought their box of treasure to the general store.

"We really did dig up all of these bottles." Laura added. "And don't you just love this skull?"

"Well," said Woody slowly, "love might not be the exact word."

"The police were terrific about Andrew," Charlie continued. "They contacted the State Department right away. Two men came to pick him up and they have already called his relatives."

"We've already made plans for a reunion at Charlie's place next month," said Laura. "We might even dress Throckmorton like a tiger again. I think he enjoyed playing that part."

"I'm trying to find out something about your bottles." Woody was thumbing through a book. "The date on them will certainly make them worth something."

"But I'm not selling the leg iron or the skull," said Charlie. "They're souvenirs."

"Do you think your mother will let you keep that skull in your house?" asked Laura.

"You bet. I might even put a plant inside it. Can't you see green leaves growing out of the eyes?"

"You're gross, Charlie. You're really gross."

"Of course, I'm not a dealer," said Woody, "but look here. According to this, an olive green bottle with a bell-bottom made around 1720 sold not long ago for $150."

"A hundred and fifty bucks apiece!" said Charlie excitedly. "Terrific! That'll be $300 for Andrew. He had a little bit of money, but this should really come in handy."

"I'm sure that bottle with the map in it is valuable to you," said Woody. "But if you are looking for a safe place to keep it, I think the museum would be happy to have it. Then you could stop by to see your treasure and everybody else could enjoy it, too."

"If they put your name on it, I want my name on

it, too," insisted Laura. "After all, I did help you find it."

"Help, nothing," argued Charlie. "If you hadn't left your tape recorder here, you wouldn't have known anything about it. You're a sneak, Laura, a sneak."

"The bottles aren't really important," Woody interrupted.

"They aren't?" said Laura.

"Not really. The map gave you a chance to help Andrew," said Woody. "That's what's really important."

"You're always right, Woody," Charlie agreed. He looked at the bottle which still held the map.

"And the best thing to do is to give it to the museum," said Laura.

"I think so," Charlie nodded. "But not right away. I might try one more time. I bet you there is still big treasure out there."